Witch

The Real Ghostbusters

Witch Way Out?

A novel by Mark Daniel

Carnival

Carnival
An imprint of the Children's Division,
part of the Collins Publishing Group,
8 Grafton Street, London W1X 3LA

Published by Carnival 1988
Reprinted 1989

Copyright © 1988 by Columbia Pictures Television,
a division of CPT Holdings, Inc.
THE REAL GHOSTBUSTERS™ Television series
Copyright © 1986 by Columbia Pictures Industries, Inc.
GHOSTBUSTERS logo and design are licensed trademarks from
Columbia Pictures Industries, Inc.

ISBN 0 00 194302 2

Printed and bound in Great Britain by
William Collins Sons & Co. Ltd, Glasgow

Chapter One

This is the story of the ghosts we could not bust.

Peter has already had a go at writing a book about our heroic activities, and the general consensus of opinion amongst The Real Ghostbusters is that, to quote Egon, our resident egghead, 'it reflected a degree of egocentricity irreconcilable with verisimilitude,' or, to quote me, it stank.

I mean, sure, he recorded what had happened in Hollywood accurately enough, but anyone reading it would have thought that he was the guy who took all the risks and made all the decisions while Ray and Egon and I just ran around getting in the way. That is Peter's trouble. Nice guy, clever enough in his way, but firmly convinced that Galileo and the rest of them got it all wrong. The solar system revolves around Peter Venkmann.

Of course, Egon is the guy who should tell our stories. The only problem is, no-one would understand a word. 'I got up and washed,' in Egonese, is 'I arose and performed my matutinal ablutions.'

Lacks punch.

As for Ray – well, Ray's too young, too keen, and anyhow he can't spell. No, what is needed is a guy who tells it like it is, who is always in the thick of the action, has a wise head on his shoulders, yet totally lacks immodesty and egotism, a guy who gives others their due. And that, as anyone who knows us will tell you, can only mean me.

Winston is the name. Winston Zeddmore. One of the Harlem Zeddmores.

OK, so I haven't got the scientific background of the others, but I reckon that sometimes that can be an advantage. Time and again when faced with unspeakable monsters, unimaginable dangers, almost certain death and things like that, Peter has been all too cool while recommending strategic retreat, Egon has been reflecting on the particular ectoplasmic structure of the troll or hobgoblin or whatever, Ray has been reminiscing about a similar case reported by Professors Fisch and Cheepz in 1921, and I have simply got on with zapping the beast. A man of few words, me. See a mess, I mop it up.

We can't of course record all our adventures, a) because the libraries would overflow and other authors could not stand the competition and would have to take up road-sweeping and b) because we'd then have no time for ghostbusting, and that would mean the end of Civilization As We Know It. All that we can do is record the really exceptional spooks for the benefit of future generations.

The spooks that I am going to tell you about were exceptional all right.

It started one dreary Sunday afternoon at the fire-station. Egon was messing about with his gadgets on the third floor while Peter, Ray, Slimer and I were enjoying a quiet hand of poker.

To be more exact, Peter and Slimer were enjoying hands of poker. I enjoyed a hand once. In March, 1979, I think it was. This was like all the other hands that I've been dealt since then. It was an unambitious sort of hand. A drop-out. It did not want to be a flush or a straight when it grew up. It did not even want to settle down to a modest way of life as a full house or two pairs. It had been a crazy mixed-up kid and it intended to stay that way. Nonetheless, ever hopeful, I had invested in its education and upbringing only to be disappointed. It would never grow up an achiever like its daddy. I disowned it. 'That's it for me,' I said sadly, 'I quit.'

Slimer bounced up and down with glee and made a noise like rusty bed-springs.

'OK, Ray,' Peter grinned and rubbed his hands gleefully above a large pile of winnings. 'What'll it be? You gonna help me make a stand against slimedom or let him bluff you out of the game?'

Ray screwed up his face in an agony of doubt.

'Come on, Ray,' Peter urged. 'You're not afraid of this bloated gooseberry, are you? I thought you had a system.'

'I have,' Ray murmured. He scrutinized his custom-built pocket calculator which would not have fitted into the pocket of a kangaroo. He stabbed at a few numbers. The printer whirred and chattered. Ray studied the print-out. 'And right now,' he sighed, 'my system is telling me to go upstairs and give Egon a hand. I'm out.'

'OK, then, green guy,' Peter sat forward grimly and looked Slimer in the eye, 'it's you and me now.'

Slimer imitated Peter. He too hunched his non-existent shoulders and studied his cards intently. 'Hmm,' he frowned deeply. He pushed forward a small part of his enormous stack of chips.

'OK,' said Peter. 'Call you and raise you double.'

Slimer considered still more deeply. His left hand now entirely covered his left eye.

'Go on,' Peter urged, 'call me, and make my year.'

I had strolled over to the 'fridge in search of food. 'Give him a minute to think about it, Peter.' I squatted and peered inside. There was nothing there save cheese and a jar of pickles clearly marked 'EGON'. 'You know Slimer doesn't respond well to pressure.' I stood and started slicing bread and cheese.

'Yeah, well,' Peter laughed, 'I'd be a lot more willing to believe that if he hadn't cleaned you two out already.'

'Oh, I'm sure he has a system,' I said, 'but it doesn't correspond to anything we humans could understand.' I looked across and suddenly saw a long green wiggly thing curling beneath the table. Something shone at its end. It emerged above the table by Peter's right arm.

Slimer's system.

Somehow, the little green slimeball had extended his eye on a long stalk like a submarine's periscope.

'Er, Peter . . .' I murmured and pointed.

He frowned and looked down. His eyes snapped open. He yelped and struck out at the eye, but Slimer was quicker. He retracted it as though it was

8

on elastic and fled with little snuffles and squeals of protest.

He perched, looking affronted, on top of one of the hi-fi speakers.

Peter grinned smugly. 'And that, gentlemen,' he scooped up all the chips and pulled them over to him, 'is my system.'

I carried the bread and cheese over to the table.

'No pickle?' asked Peter.

'Yeah, but Egon's marked the jar "Egon".'

'Forget that,' Peter stood and marched to the 'fridge. 'Do I go round marking all my stuff? All for one and one for all, that's my policy.'

He spread the six sandwiches with the thick, chunky dark pickle, and for a while there was no sound save that of contented munching. Evening closed in. Slimer grabbed one sandwich and inhaled it. Peter cursed him and threw a book at him. Ordinary, peaceful domestic life.

Egon and Ray came down and joined us. Egon walked straight to the 'fridge and asked if anyone had seen the particularly revolting mould that he had been developing in a jar there. Peter turned almost as green as Slimer. Even Slimer said 'Yech!'

I was making my way rapidly to the toilet when Egon revealed that it had been, after all, what he called a 'humorous entertainment'.

Astonishing, the things which amuse some people.

It was about then that Janine came in from next door. 'We've got a client,' she said in a crisp monotone, and somehow she contrived to apply lipstick at the same time. 'Name; Armour, Sylvia. Doctor.

Rich. Widow. Serious out of control spooks running amok throughout her apartment block. All her tenants having coronaries, hysterics etcetera. Sounds urgentish.'

'We're already there,' I told her.

We weren't, of course, as Peter was quick to point out in his usual sarky way, but it took a mere two minutes to strap on our proton packs, slither down the fireman's pole, pile into Ecto 1, our custom-converted ambulance, and, with a couple of dramatic backfires, roar – well, cough – out on to the streets. We made it to Dr Armour's place in just under twenty minutes.

Chapter Two

It was almost dark as we stepped out on to the sidewalk beneath a burly-looking block of flats. Its once white windows were now yellowish and flaking. They stared dolefully down on the street like drunkards' eyes. A rickety fire-escape crisscrossed the façade like a singularly methodical snake. The whole effect was of derelict respectability – the sort of joint where they have blood feuds over bridge-games, and people get a whole lot more pleasure out of not talking to their neighbours than they ever could out of talking to them.

A very thin, gaunt woman in a floral printed frock and a tatty woollen coat stood wringling her hands on the doorstep. She was perhaps fifty, fifty-five. It was difficult to tell. She was fine-featured and had obviously once been attractive, but there were bags beneath her eyes and the lines from her nose to the corners of her mouth were etched deep in her dry white skin.

'Mrs Armour?' Peter held out a hand. She took it eagerly. 'We're The Real Ghostbusters, at your service.'

'That's right,' I added, 'show us your ghouls and we'll just gobble 'em up for you. Spectral spring cleanin's our game.'

'Thank God!' Sylvia Armour breathed, 'I've been waiting . . .'

'No significant PKE,' Egon twanged at my right shoulder. PKE for those younger readers who haven't got that far in school, stands for Psycho-Kinetic Energy. You get a lot of it when there are spooks about.

'Curious,' said Peter. 'Now Dr Armour, what can you tell us?'

'Oh, dear,' she flapped, 'I don't know where to start.'

'A problem that even we writers have sometimes, my dear,' Peter soothed. There'll be a little less of the 'we writers' stuff when *this* book starts picking up the literary prizes.

'I'd ask you in,' Dr Armour glanced over her shoulder, 'only I don't dare go in there myself. All my tenants have gone and they've refused to pay rent. I don't blame them, but it's my only source of income.'

'You're retired, then?' I asked.

'No!' she frowned. 'Oh, I see! The "doctor", you mean. No, I'm not a doctor of medicine. I'm a historian. I've been writing a book for the last twelve years.'

'Big book,' said Peter resentfully. 'So, just tell us where these spooks came from and what they've been up to, and everything'll be back to normal in no time.'

'They wail,' she shuddered, 'they wail and moan and bang things and knock things over.'

'Male or female?' I asked.

'Female, I think,' she said. 'Three or four of them by the sound of it. They sound so unhappy.'

12

'You haven't seen them, then?'

'No. No, I've heard them, and felt them. Yesterday two of them grabbed my hands and pulled me up the stairs. It was – it was a horrifying experience. They were shrieking and I couldn't see them and I was struggling and screaming but they just dragged me bumping up all the stairs.'

'You don't know where they were taking you?'

'No,' she ran a fluttering hand through her iron grey hair. 'I managed to break free from them on the landing.'

'How long have you had them, Dr Armour?' Egon demanded.

'About – about ten days,' she said softly. She looked down at her clasped hands.

'So why didn't you call us before?'

'I – I know I should have done,' she sighed. She blinked up at the cloudy grey sky. 'I just hoped they'd go away. I didn't want to create a fuss.'

THIS WAS WRONG. I don't want to lecture, but it's an important point. If you get ghosts, don't delay. Don't worry about false alarms. Don't feel embarrassed. Call us. We'd rather be called and discover that there's no problem than come too late. End of lecture.

'No psychic emanations before that?' asked Peter.

She shook her head. 'No. It's always been a happy house.'

'OK, Dr Armour. Don't worry about a thing. Those ghouls don't know it, but they're as good as history. Have you got a friend nearby that you can stay with while we're in there? We might be some time.'

'Yes,' she shivered, this time, I think, from cold. 'I'll go down and see my friends the Greys. They live in the basement apartment next door.'

'See you there. Ready, guys?'

We unslung our proton guns. 'Ready.'

'You will take care, won't you?' Dr Armour pleaded to our backs.

'Ma'am,' I assured her over my shoulder, 'relax. You are talking to The Real Ghostbusters. OK, guys,' I said, 'let's go.'

Chapter Three

Everything looked grey inside, even when we had
switched on the light. Dusk gathered in the corners
and laid dust on the table in the hallway. It was a
high-ceilinged room and once it had been grand.
The walls were pale blue. There were ornate white
mouldings at the cornices and at the centre of the
ceiling. Again, however, the paint was flaking. The
mirror above the table was mottled like an old man's
skin, and Egon's eyes lit up at the spattering of grey-
green fungus in one corner.

We clattered across the tiled floor to the door on
the right. It opened on a gloomy apartment which,
like the hall, was down at heel but could have told
you a thing or two about the high life. Someone had
left in a hurry. The wastepaper-bins were full. Paper-
back books lay scattered on the floor. The bed – the
big, old-fashioned mahogany variety that you need a
Sherpa guide to get on to – was stripped. Horsehair
sprouted from the mattress.

'PKE reading?' barked Peter.

'Next to nothing,' Egon replied.

We inspected the kitchen and the bathroom. Still
no sign of spooks. In the other ground floor flat it
was the same story. Signs of recent habitation. No
PKE.

'OK, upstairs.' Peter swung round on his heel and
led us back out into the hall. It's ridiculous the way

that he thinks he's boss, but I must admit that he can be quite impressive at times.

The first floor also yielded nothing, though in one of the two apartments there were broken vases and glasses, proof either of the tenants' panic or of the ghosts' vandalism.

We climbed another flight. The staircarpets were threadbare and our footfalls slapped at the high ceiling and echoed in the walls. Spooky, but still no spooks.

'This is ridiculous,' Ray shook his head. 'I mean, we must get *some* reading.'

'Uh-uh,' Egon frowned. 'Not a thing. Possibly a spook cockroach or two, but, if anything, below average for a house this age.'

'So what's happening, for the Lord's sake?'

Egon shrugged. 'Makes no sense to me.'

That was when the fun started.

The lights flickered twice and went out. There was still a little cool blue light from the streetlamp below which gave the room an eerie underwater quality.

'Power failure?' murmured Peter.

I fumbled for my flashlight, but before I could get it out, a deep, guttural moan shook the floorboards. It was answered by another from above, another from somewhere outside in the stairwell.

'Spectro-visors,' cried Peter above the noise. The spectro-visor is one of Egon's cleverest gadgets. It enables you to see otherwise invisible ghosts.

Usually.

It didn't work this time. Though the moaning

16

continued and seemed to come from a spot only inches away, we could see no-one.

There were heavy thuds on the bare boards upstairs. They sounded like an Arctic explorer's last dragged and weary footfalls. The moans mounted in pitch and became shrill wails.

'Still no reading?' Peter yelled.

Egon shook his head, bemused. His whole ordered world had turned upside down.

'Come on!' I called. 'Let's try up there!'

We charged out into the stairwell again and took the steps three at a time. We were in a dark, musty corridor lined with tiny attic rooms. Servants' quarters, presumably, a long time ago. The wailing up here was very close and very loud, and there was a new sound too, accompanying the heavy footfalls ahead of us.

The clanking of chains.

'Oh, no!' Peter cried as he ran down the corridor at our head. 'How hammy can you get? Wailing, moaning and the clanking of chains went out with the ark, girls! Times have . . .' Then he screamed.

He stopped so suddenly that we all piled up behind him. 'What is it, Peter?' asked Ray.

Peter stood absolutely still. His face was drained of blood. 'I – am – being – held – here,' he croaked, struggling for each word. 'There are four arms holding mine.'

Ray leaned forward. He reached out and ran his hand through the air around Peter's right arm. The hand stopped and darted back as though burned. Ray too was very pale, his eyes wide as he turned to

17

us. 'It's – it's true,' he gasped. 'There's someone there . . .'

'But there's still no PKE!' Egon sounded almost irritated. 'It doesn't make sense!'

'"There are more things on heaven and earth . . ."' Peter began huskily.

He stopped and at the same moment I span around, my proton-gun at my hip. Up the stairs which we had just climbed, snuffling and moaning and dragging its chains, another spook trudged, cutting off all retreat. It reached the top and came wearily on down the corridor. Its invisible footfalls came nearer and nearer.

'Blast it, Winston!' Ray squeaked behind me.

I fired, spraying the corridor with high-energy ions. The fusillade lit up the corridor like a continous lightning flash. It should have had any self-respecting ghoul howling with pain and retreating fast.

Not this one. It just came on.

Something pushed my gun aside. I backed up against the other Ghostbusters. Something that felt exactly like a hand pushed at my chest. It was my turn to yelp.

I reached out for the place where there should have been an arm. There was an arm, clad in some loose flowing fabric. I followed it up to an unquestionable shoulder, then the soft skin of a female face.

'Egon . . .' I said weakly. 'Do something . . .'

'I think,' muttered Peter, 'that we are in trouble.'

There was a moan from the she-spook that held me. I could feel the warmth of her breath. One of her pals moaned back. Not exactly renowned for witty chat, ghosts.

'What do you want?' Peter called loudly. His voice came back to us in receding waves, rattling the old boards and making the stone walls sing.

There was silence for a minute or two, then, in a deep voice, one of Peter's captors answered. She forced out each word as though it took an immense physical effort. She had trouble with her consonants too. It sounded a bit like someone on her deathbed trying to speak immortal last words through a ventriloquist's dummy. 'Cub wizh ush,' she croaked.

'Come with you, where?'

'Back! Cub wizh ush back!'

'Back to where you came from?'

'Yesh,' she moaned.

'OK,' Peter shrugged, 'show us where you came from.'

'Not *where*,' she said slowly as though the record were running down, 'Whed.'

'*When?*' Peter frowned. 'You mean, back in time?'

'Yesh.'

'Uh-oh,' said Peter.

Chapter Four

They were quite nice really, once you got to know them. I mean, they let us go, which was good of them, on condition that we would come back. They were most insistent about that bit.

Not that we had much choice. I mean, it is not in a Ghostbuster's nature to allow spooks to run around unchecked, whatever the cost in terms of personal danger and suffering. If we'd walked away and stayed away, *we* would have been OK, but Dr Armour's house would have remained uninhabited and she would have remained penniless. We couldn't have that.

We have chosen (here, by the way, comes a piece of writing to knock Peter's socks off), we have chosen to chart this perilous course through life's rough waters and have no-one but ourselves to blame. Let others lie basking and becalmed in the shallows. Our endless journey takes us by unknown coral reefs and rocky shores, through the hurricane's blast and the roar of the storm. Fortune's tides throw us up high and cast us down low, but we do not heed the murmurings of our faint hearts. Duty, we know, bids us to sail onward, ever onward, through whatever perils may lie in our way, unblenching and unbowed.

Thank you.

It was raining by the time that we stepped out into the street again. The pavements shone.

'The thing about those spooks,' said Egon, 'is that they are not spooks.'

'What are you on about?' I asked.

'They are not, strictly speaking, ghosts. They do not give off Psycho-Kinetic Energy. They cannot be seen with the Spectro-Visors. The proton-guns don't work against them, and I'm prepared to bet that the ghost traps won't either.'

'So what are they?' Peter demanded. 'Figments of our imagination? 'Cos, if so, they're the solidest figments my imagination's ever had.'

'No, no. They're real, OK, but I think we've probably come across a door in the space-time continuum. It does happen,' he said casually.

A truck rumbled by, causing us all to perform an intricate and agile dance in order to avoid the wave of water that spurted from its wheels. We cursed a bit and wrung out our trouser-cuffs. When we had settled down, Egon continued. 'You see, ghosts are defunct, right? They die, and their spirits pass beyond the ecto-barrier, but some, usually for reasons of malice, find holes in the ecto-barrier and return to haunt the living, right?'

'Skip the high-school stuff,' Peter sighed. 'I am getting wet.'

'OK. Well – I'm not sure about this, but I think – I think that these are the spirits of people who are, in a manner of speaking, still alive. I mean, they're dead in our time, but in their own time they're alive and suffering some intense emotional disturbance.

They project their need for help in quasi-corporeal form, and by some chance those projections find a door in the space-time continuum which leads them into the here and now. But the people projecting those projections are still alive and in trouble in their own time, if you see what I mean.'

'No,' I shrugged.

'I think I get you,' Peter nodded. 'You mean, if I'm in big trouble, it's theoretically possible for me to send out a sort of spiritual message and you guys would receive it by hearing it or feeling it or perhaps seeing an image of me.'

'Certainly,' Egon nodded.

'But because that call for help has no mass, like ectoplasm, it can easily shift from one age to another, and some guy who isn't yet born might hear me shouting "Help!"'

'Or some person who is long dead,' amended Egon. 'It works both ways. I mean, for all we know, Napoleon lost the battle of Waterloo because he was distracted by a projection of you crying for help just at the crucial moment.'

'So you're saying,' Ray frowned deeply, 'that what we met up with there were really *thoughts*.'

'That's right. And because those thoughts happen to have ended up on our patch, we have to go back and help their thinkers, otherwise they'll just keep on moaning and making a nuisance of themselves forever.'

'Wow!' said Ray reverently. 'This is great!'

I had not contributed much to this conversation, as you will have noticed. That is because I was thinking deeply. Deep Thinkers do keep quiet, I find. It is also because Egon does not speak clearly and a car passed just at the moment when he said that bit about 'quasi-corporeal'. I thought he said 'quasi-corporal' and was trying to work out whether it meant 'almost a non-commissioned officer', as in waiting for promotion, or 'a half-sized non-commissioned officer,' as in Napoleon (see above) – and what non-commissioned officers had to do with the ghosts, or rather non-ghosts, in the attic.

Natural enough mistake. Could happen to anyone. And anyhow, what does a guy want to go round talking like a dictionary for?

'So where – or rather when – do you think we have to go?' I asked.

'That,' said Peter grimly, 'is what we're about to find out. It's time we had a serious word with the good Dr Armour. I'll do the talking. We doctors, you know . . .'

The temptation to kick Peter is sometimes overwhelming.

'Now, Dr Armour,' Dr Peter Venkmann stood steaming before the roaring gas fire in the basement apartment. 'You haven't told us everything, have you?'

'I – I think so,' she blinked nervously up at him. 'Everything relevant, at least. You mean – you haven't got rid of them?'

'Not yet, but we will. When did you first hear these spectres, Dr Armour?'

'I told you. About ten days ago.'

'And what were you doing at the time?'

'I was working.' she sipped her tea.

'And your field of study?'

'Seventeenth-century America.'

'Or, more exactly . . .'

'Residual Vestiges of North European Superstition, Myth and Ritual in Colonial Massachussets.'

Peter gulped, blinked and said, 'Ah!' as if that explained everything.

Egon sat down and eyed Dr Armour with something approaching affection. Anyone who could spend twelve years studying all that, his expression seemed to say, must be all right.

'And what, precisely, were you doing when first you heard the ghosts? I want you to think very carefully, Dr Armour.'

She stood. The teacup rattled a little on the saucer as she walked across the room to study a picture of a very long thin horse. She sighed. 'I don't have to think carefully,' she said, 'I was reading a rare manuscript. An original, eye-witness account of the Salem witch-trials written by Dr Piet Vansittart, the chief witchhunter.'

Peter looked at Egon and nodded.

Egon nodded back. Ray nodded sagely to himself. Everyone was doing it, so I nodded a bit too.

'Have you got that manuscript here?' asked Egon.

'No, but I have a transcript.' She delved deep into a huge handbag. 'Here we are. Yes. It was about here. It reads – ahem . . . *"and Seth Goodbody the gaoler relates that the three wantons; Jocasta Martin,*

Tabitha Carter and Molly Lovejoy did last night much dissemble grief and pleaded most dolefully, protesting that they were innocent of evildoing and of the practice of the dark arts, the which Seth knew to be false even as the words fell from their lips, for Jocasta Martin spake in a deep voice not her own, saying over and over, 'It is not fair!' which is to say, 'It is dark', for all which is not fair is dark, and thus is she contemned out of her own mouth, the while Tabitha Carter wept copious tears which were seen to give off vapour as they fell upon the stone floor, and thus is contemned, and Molly Lovejoy spake thus, saying, 'an we were sorceresses, would we not command the doors to open and fly free from this cell?' which twice contemns her a sorceress, for first, she reveals her knowledge of witches' methods of escape, and second, such argument is too devious to come of mortal reasoning . . ." That,' Dr Armour laid down the paper, 'is what I was reading when the moaning started. Terrible, isn't it?'*

'Appalling,' said Peter, 'he should keep his sentences shorter.'

'No, but those poor girls,' Ray sniffed. 'I mean, if you say it's not fair, you're a witch, if your tears steam, you're a witch, if you say something sensible, you're a witch.'

'That's right,' Dr Armour nodded, 'and if you talked gibberish, you were possessed by the devil and so were a witch.'

'Well,' Egon polished his glasses, 'looks like we've found our spooks.'

'Yup,' Peter turned to Dr Armour. 'What time of year was that written?' he asked.

'December.'

'Oh, great. Could it be June in Florida? Christmas in Hawaii? Paris in the springtime? Oh, no. Massachussets in December. Thanks a lot.'

'You mean, these poor girls are causing all that trouble in my house?' Dr Armour frowned.

'Yup, but they don't know that they are,' explained Egon. 'Somehow what you read – did you read it aloud by any chance?'

'Yes, I'm afraid I did.'

'Somehow those girls' pleas for mercy took shape and came here to seek help, perhaps because you are the first person since then to have spoken that form of words. We've got to go back with them and see if we can help them.'

'Back to Salem?' she started.

'Yup. Have you any record as to what happened to those particular girls?'

'No,' she smiled, 'they were the last recorded people to be arrested for witchcraft. After that, the madness seems to have passed. But whether they escaped or were executed, we just don't know. But hold it,' she said firmly, 'if you're going to Salem, I'm coming with you.'

'Sorry, ma'am,' I told her, 'No go. We're gonna have enough on our hands without having you to worry about. The Ghostbusters go in alone.'

'But think what I could learn . . .'

'We'll report back to you, ma'am,' said Peter crisply. 'Sorry, but this is a job for experts.'

'Oh, yeah,' she said surprisingly, 'and what do you know about seventeenth century Massachussets?'

'Well . . .' Peter waggled his open hand dubiously. 'Nothing, right?'

'Oh, I wouldn't say *nothing* exactly. Not much, I grant you.'

'Sit down,' she said, 'and pin back your ears.'

Chapter Five

It was nearly midnight when we again let ourselves
into Dr Armour's house. The lights were still not
working and the rooms looked larger and emptier
than ever in the pitch blackness. Our flashlight
beams swang this way and that like duelling sabres.
Every sound seemed unnaturally loud – the rustle of
our clothes, the rattle of our equipment, the hollow
thumping of our boots on the bare boards.

At the top of the topmost flight, an invisible hand
grasped my wrist and gently pulled me towards the
first of the rooms along the corridor. It was a small
square room with nothing in it save a tatty, tiled
fireplace, a rolled up rug and a long, low oak chest.
Our guides crooned like contented pigeons as they
urged us towards the chest.

'What worries me,' whispered Ray, 'is how do
we know what we're going to find when we get
there?'

'We don't,' I answered, 'so we'd better keep the
flashlights off.'

'Why are we whispering?' Ray asked as the lid of
the oak chest was lifted by unseen hands.

'I don't know,' Peter whispered back. 'OK, guys.
See you three hundred years ago.' He swung first
one leg, then another, over the edge of the chest
and, like a diver descending from a boat, sank slowly
into the darkness.

I went next. I too swung both legs into the chest and sat perched for a moment on the wooden edge. My feet did not touch the ground, and a cold wind blew about my legs. I turned to face the room and lowered myself slowly down, feeling for a foothold.

I did not find one until I was almost at full stretch. My boots scraped on rough stone and slowly I transferred my weight to my feet. I could see nothing and the cold wind whipped about me. I looked up, expecting to see the flashlight beams above me. There was nothing but deep darkness.

'Peter?' I called softly. There was no reply. Tentatively, I reached out a foot. It touched nothing. This was worrying, since I had no idea whether the drop was one of six inches or six hundred feet. I turned round, laid my fists on the stone where I was standing, let my right foot down.

It was six inches.

I was on some sort of crude staircase. I felt my way slowly down. Above me, consolingly, I heard another pair of boots grating on the stone.

I nearly fell over when I discovered that I was on flat ground. Something rustled in front of me. 'Hi,' I whispered, straining my eyes to see in the darkness, 'Peter?'

'Ho,' Peter called softly, a few feet away to my left. I felt my way towards him with outstretched hands. I touched something soft. Whatever it was yapped and pulled away fast.

'Over here,' Peter said again. This time, my fingers fumbled at the reassuring moulded glass-fibre of a proton-pack.

'We are not alone,' Peter whispered.

'Is this the time for eternal truths?'

'No, I mean *here*.'

'Yeah. Realized that. I just squeezed a seventeenth century arm that felt surprisingly warm.'

'Don't talk about warm, Winston,' Peter shivered. 'What's that word mean, anyhow? Minor memory lapse.'

'Me too,' I stamped. 'I'm *freezing*.'

'Hey, guys!' called a husky voice.

'Yeah. Over here to your left,' I called back. Someone behind me whimpered, a quick little whiplash of sound. Again, something rustled.

'Hi. That you, Winston?' Ray's hand clasped my shoulder.

'Yeah. And Peter.'

'Phew! Can we switch on a flashlight or something?'

'No. Hold it,' Peter muttered. 'Let's wait till Egon gets here, then we'll talk it over.'

Egon arrived a minute later. There was still more whimpering and rustling. 'It is a trifle cold,' Egon said.

'A trifle?' I squeaked. 'What you talkin' about, man? It is, at the very least, a baked-Alaska-cold, before the baking . . .'

Something scuttled at my feet. I stiffened. My voice at last came out like that of a speak-your-weight machine, 'Whassat?'

'What's what?'

'There are things,' I droned, 'or rather animals, running over my feet.'

'Ah, yes,' Egon said calmly, '*rattus norvegicus* or *rattus rattus*. Impossible to tell which in this light. Probably *rattus rattus* or the black rat, which is smaller and less aggressive than its brown cousin.'

'Oh,' I gulped, not much consoled.

'. . . though of course it is notorious for its role in carrying plague.'

'Oh,' I whimpered almost as high as our invisible friends behind us.

'Er, do you think we could have some light?'

'Reckon so,' Peter's teeth chattered, 'but just the one flashlight. We still don't know where we are.'

There was a click, then three shrill little yelps of horror from the corner. The torch beam showed grey walls streaked with green and glistening with slime. It also showed a thick dark simmering liquid which bubbled and spread over the rough stone floor. Rats. Not just one or two, but a whole host of the things, all squeaking and scuttling. Icy oil wriggled down my spine. Suddenly I felt very sick.

The beam of light swung upward. It showed three pairs of bare and dirty feet, three ragged skirts, three young and frankly terrified faces framed by wild and matted hair. One had red hair, one blonde, one glossy black. All three girls had covered their eyes with their arms and clung to one another, trying, so it seemed, to push their way into the solid stone of the walls.

'It's OK,' said Ray softly. 'Don't be frightened.' He took a step forward. The girls whimpered and trembled.

31

'We know who you are,' Peter soothed. 'We've come to help you.'

'Holy Mary, mother of God, pray for us sinners . . .' the girl with red hair crossed herself. The others joined in her mumbling, '. . . now, and at the hour of our death . . .'

'*Rattus rattus*,' droned Egon dreamily, 'I thought so.'

We ignored him. 'Look, girls,' I said. 'We haven't got much time if we're to help you. At least look at us. We're not monsters, we're not ghosts, we're real people.'

'Er, Winston,' said Peter drily.

'Yup?'

'They can't look at us because the flashlight is shining at them and we're in darkness. Tell you what. Why doesn't one of you go over there and shine your flashlight on me?'

'Whyn't you go, Peter?' I demanded.

'Because,' he shrugged, 'we are trying to reassure these poor girls, not frighten them out of their wits. They need to see a face in which courage is mingled with compassion, strength with sensitivity, wisdom with winsomeness . . .'

I couldn't stand much more of this. 'All right,' I broke in, 'all right.'

I tiptoed over the rats to the far wall and shone my flashlight at Peter, Egon and Ray. 'Now,' I said, 'please at least look at us. We're humans, just like you.'

The redhead lowered her arm for a second, took

one quick look at Peter, gave a little shriek and went back to praying again.

'OK,' said Peter with surprising sternness, 'I've had enough of this. Come along, girls, stand up straight and look at us. We have come here to deliver you from imprisonment and see that justice is done. You have a simple choice. Either you pluck up your courage and help us, or you stand in the corner whimpering like whipped dogs, in which case we can do nothing for you and you will go to the gallows as witches. Make up your minds.'

Chapter Six

The redhead slowly released her hold on her blonde friend and straightened. She blinked at us with wide grey eyes.

She was very tall. 'I know not,' she said in a deep, husky voice, 'whence ye come nor what dark magic has summoned ye hither, but ye speak of justice, so I am prepared to heed ye.'

'Good of you,' said Peter. 'Come on, and you other two.'

The blonde girl opened her eyes. She too straightened. She was very small and slight. She cowered nervously behind her older, bolder friend. The last girl stepped forward more brazenly. She had glittering dark eyes, full lips and a voluptuous figure.

'Why look ye so strange and wear such outlandish apparel?' she demanded.

'We come from another age,' explained Egon. 'Your sorrowing has summoned us hither to assist you.'

'Thy speech is fair, sir,' said the redhead, 'unlike the crude tongue which thy fellows speak.'

'What the heck is she rapping on about?' Peter was affronted. 'Crude speech? Me?'

I shared his concern. 'You mean we've come to a place where everyone talks like Egon all the time?'

'Yeah, well,' Peter shrugged, 'it's not their fault.

They've only had a hundred and fifty years or so to learn proper English.'

'I thought they came from England,' Ray frowned.

'Yeah, maybe, but that's the point. You ever heard an Englishman trying to speak English? No can do. Let's have some introductions around here. Which of you girls is which?'

'I,' pronounced the redhead, 'am Jocasta Martin.'

'I'm Molly Lovejoy,' the dark girl mustered a smile.

'And I . . .' the little blonde squeaked, gave up, fluttered her eyelashes a few times and flung her grubby apron over her head.

'You're Tabitha Carter, right?'

'She is,' confirmed Jocasta. 'Silly chit.'

'Can you explain to us what's been happening here?' I asked, still staring nervously down at the rats.

'It is maintained that we are sorceresses, practitioners of the dark arts and servants of Satan. If the case against us be proven, we shall be condemned to death, as many of our sisters have already been.'

'What evidence have they?' asked Egon.

'They need but little evidence, for the whole town is gripped by fear and righteous anger, and the least suspicion is sufficient to send an innocent man to the gallows.'

'So what started all this?'

'There have been strange manifestations and apparitions in many of the houses in Salem. Profane voices have sounded at church services and the bells have rung in the night, pulled by unseen hands.

Inanimate objects have flown through the air, and footfalls have been heard in many an empty upper room.'

'Sounds like spooks to me.' Peter expressed what we were all feeling.

'Wouldst interpret thy friend's uncouth ramblings?' asked Molly.

Egon obliged. 'He means,' he said, 'that such manifestations are more commonly indicative of the mischievous antics of phantoms than of sorcery.'

'Yes. For all that he gibbers like an idiot, thy friend speaks sooth.'

'Could we leave out this "gibbering" stuff?' Peter snapped. 'I'm beginning to think I should have stayed in New York.'

'Where is this "New York"?' asked Molly.

'I don't believe this!' Peter squeaked. 'Where is New York? Where is the sun? New York is only the centre of the Universe, Ma'am.'

'It hasn't even been invented, Peter,' Egon explained.

'Ah, so this is prehistory. Right.'

'Can we return to the subject, please?' Egon blinked. 'So why did your community start looking for witches rather than common-or-garden ghosts?'

Molly shook her head. 'Pastor Kraft claims that there are no such things as ghosts and that it is sacrilege to speak of them.'

'Pastor Kraft sounds like a right jerk to me,' said Peter.

'What says your drivelling friend?'

'He opines that Pastor Kraft is mayhap a dolt and a poltroon.'

'Extraordinary, the wisdom that can come from the lips of the afflicted,' said Jocasta. 'Pastor Kraft, then, is indeed a jerk. He is a paragon of jerkdom. Though it ill befits me to speak ill of a man of God, yet doth his jerkishness far surpass that of all other jerks that I have encountered.'

'Right,' I said. 'I assume, from the company that you are keeping and from the lack of central heating, that you would like to get out of here. Shall we blast down the door?'

'No!' gasped Jocasta. 'No! We must stay here!'

'What? Why?'

'Dost thou not see? If we should escape by whatever magic is at your command, the case against us will be proven! They will aver that ye are imps of Satan and that we have conjured ye by witchcraft! If there is aught that ye can do to prove the justice of our cause, ye must do it without us.'

'And ye must find a more suitable garb than yon masquerade costumes. If they see ye thus attired, ye will be imprisoned at once.'

'I'd like to see 'em try.'

I spoke bullishly, but Molly corrected me.

'Nay,' she purred. 'Dost thou not see? Whatever you do must have nothing of magic about it, else we'll burn for sure. Ye must appear to be ordinary mortal men. And it were as well that your friend should not talk,' she nodded at Peter. 'His uncouth manner of speech would give ye away at once.'

Peter's fists clenched. His shoulders shook. He

37

seemed to be turning pink. He gargled for a while, but all that he could say was 'I . . . I . . . I . . .'

'Yes,' Jocasta nodded, 'much better that he keeps his mouth shut.'

'So where do we find these more suitable clothes?' I demanded.

Jocasta ran a long white hand through her mane of red hair. 'My husband,' she said, 'is a Tailor, Draper, Hosier and Gents' Outfitter, patronized by the Nobility and the Gentry, Surgical Trusses and Outsized Jockey Shorts a speciality. Go hence to the fourth house on the right as you emerge from the prison-house. Give this ring to him as a token of good faith. It is our wedding ring, so guard it well. He will clothe you. But until then, beware that none should see you.'

'OK. Now. If we're not gonna blast the door, will someone tell me how we get outta here?' Peter was seething.

'Easy,' said Ray. He strolled over to the big, studded oak door and squinted quickly into the keyhole. He did Something Quick and Proficient with a bit of metal. There was a rasping, grinding sound, a clunk, and the door swung inward.

'How do you do things like that?' I shook my head admiringly.

'Sh!' whispered Molly. 'Seth Goodbody is out there. He will be drunk, of course, but tread lightly.'

'We shall,' Egon whispered back, 'and cease your weeping, ladies. There is no longer cause for you to vex your hearts. The Ghostbusters are here, and they're on your side.'

Chapter Seven

We closed the door quietly behind us and Ray did the same Something Quick and Proficient backwards. The corridor in which we stood was no better than the cell. The walls were pock-marked and grey. There was a strong smell of damp and fungus and a few other undesirable things.

We tiptoed down the corridor towards the door at the end. Peter switched off his flashlight, hushed us, then slowly pushed open the door.

A single candle lit the small room into which we stepped. There was nothing in there save a big black carved table, a big black chair, a big black bottle and a big man with a huge black beard, a large paunch and very hairy fingers. Together they took up all but a few inches of the room. The man inhaled with a noise like water going down the plug, exhaled with a whistle and a series of moist chewing noises. We squeezed past him to the door.

Outside, the sky was clear and the moon was bright. The wooden houses of the main street were dabbed and streaked with pale purple light. The cart ruts in the dirt were like long black coils of rope. At another time, the whole scene would have reminded me of a Christmas card. I would have paused to breathe in the Olde Worlde Charm and my heart would have been warmed by the uncorrupted innocence and simplicity of our pilgrim fathers' way of life. At that moment, however, nothing less than four minutes at 'defrost' in the microwave could have warmed my heart or any other part of me. I had no care for the beauty of the scene. All that I wanted was a warm bath and a warm bed.

Strange, this matter of beauty. (Wake up out there. Here comes the Philosophical Bit which will really knock 'em dead when they hand out the book prizes.) I mean, poets have striven to find the precisely perfect pattern of words to elevate our thoughts to Higher Things, yet we have all known moments when the words 'Public Toilet' or 'Pizza Parlour' are more beautiful, moving and affecting than any Shakespeare sonnet. In fact, come to think of it, the words 'Public Toilet' are probably the most beautiful words in the world, in that everyone has at one time or another found them irresistible, while not everyone has read Shakespeare's sonnets. Me included.

In much the same way, the beauty of a simple colonial seventeenth century street in the moonlight with a wisp of snow in the air would have been immediately obvious to me if I had just eaten a steak, medium rare, with french fries and a side salad and had then turned out for a stroll with my friends. But, standing there with my teeth chattering, uncertain as to whether my extremities really were still mine and acutely aware that, if we were seen, we and our new friends would probably be burned (not an unattractive thought considering the temperature) to death (not so good), I was blind to Salem's charms.

All of which goes to prove Zeddmore's first principle: all good, pure thoughts depend upon a full stomach, an empty bladder and a warm coat.

Jacob Carter's place was a long, low two-storey house of white clapboard. There were no neon signs to show the nature of the business, just a small copper-plate scroll above the door. 'Jacob Carter,' it said, 'Taylor, Draper, Hofier and Gentf Outfitterf, patronifed by ye Nobilitye and ye Gentry. Furgical Truffef and Outfized Jockey Fhortf a fpecialitye.'

'Either Jocasta or the signwriter's got a speech impediment,' said Peter. He tapped on the door.

A little man with a bristling white moustache opened it almost at once. He wore a white nightshirt and a floppy nightcap. 'I'm so sorry,' he bleated. 'I came down for a book. I'll be just a second.' He shut the door in Peter's face.

We heard him galloping up the stairs. Peter knocked on the door again. A moment later, the window above was opened and the little man leaned out. 'What is it?' he scowled.

'We've got a secret message from your wife,' Egon stage-whispered.

'Do you know what time it is?'

'Yes. I'm sorry, but it's a matter of life and death.'

'I don't know what's wrong with the youth of today. Can't a man get a decent night's sleep? Life and death, you say? Very well, very well. I'm coming.'

The window shut. We heard him trudging back down the stairs, grumbling as he went. Bolts were shot. Chains rattled. The door opened.

'Sorry about that,' he bleated, 'but we must observe Life's little proprieties, hmm? Come in, and welcome, brethren. I don't know why we say that, because you're not my brethren of course. Don't look a bit like me. Don't look much like human beings, come to that. Still, it's the done thing. Everyone's your brother or your sister these days. Makes things complicated. Wooing, for example. "Wilt thou marry me, sister?" "Yes, brother." Sounds odd. Then there's "Hast thou another brother, brother?" and "Hast seen my sister, sister?" "Yea, thou hast just missed 'er, sister." Confusing. Still, this is the seventeenth century. One must move with the times. I don't suppose ye'd like a goblet of piping hot mulled wine, would ye? You would? Oh, good. Now, what was it you wanted . . ?'

He carried on in this vein for some five minutes before we could get a word in edgeways. Occasionally he offered to build up the fire or to give us food and drink. Then he would get distracted and forget all about it.

Eventually we managed to persuade him to sit down. Ray built the fire. Peter raided the kitchen and brought back a ham and some warm ale and some things in breadcrumbs (which turned out, so the old man said, to be hogs' cheeks), and we explained our mission to him.

'Well,' he said. 'Well well well well well. This is exciting. From another century, eh? Well, well.

Never know who you're going to meet next, eh? And you need clothes? Quite right. Everyone needs clothes. Cold without 'em. Well, I'm sure I've got some old garments which will fit. People don't pay their bills, you know, and then I'm left with all these suits. Can't wear 'em all myself, can I? Just the thing for ye. May be a bit old-fashioned, but there we are. Hold on a second. I'll go and fetch 'em for ye.'

He pottered off towards the back of the house. 'He doesn't seem a bit surprised to see us,' whispered Ray.

'I know,' Peter rubbed his hands over the fire. 'I think he's a little screwy.'

The old man returned with his arms full of black fabric. 'Extraordinary thing,' he beamed, 'they were exactly where I'd left 'em. Don't expect that, do you?'

'Er . . ., no,' we frowned and smiled soothingly at the same time.

Screwy he may have been, but he still had a tailor's eye. The clothes fitted perfectly, and soon we were preening ourselves in black gaiters and knickerbockers, black tunics with white linen collars and black wide-brimmed hats.

'Who died?' asked Peter.

'Oh, no, no,' the old man remonstrated. 'No, when in mourning, one wears the black collar. This is normal day dress. The fashion, you know. One must do the right thing. I'm afraid that thou,' he smoothed down Ray's collar, 'mayst be thought a trifle frivolous. Thou wilt notice that the lining of thy tunic is grey, but then, as I said, some of these

43

garments are very old, and we were more dashing in those days. Reckless, even. I once,' he giggled coyly, 'had a red kerchief. Sinfully indulgent, but such fun. In private only, of course.'

'Of course.' Egon nodded seriously. 'Have we thy permission, sir, to stay here until morning?'

'Yes! Yes indeed! Eat, drink and be merry. Oh, I do like curling up with a good dream like this, especially when it involves food, eh? I can eat as much as I like and tomorrow the food will still be there to be eaten all over again! Wonderful! And people from another century – well, it beats reality any old day, I say. In the old days, I'd've told 'em all about it down at the tavern tomorrow. Nowadays of course, it's not allowed. I'd be had up for a warlock and hanged, like as not. It's that Piet Vansittart and his Witchhunters. They see witches and warlocks everywhere. Did I tell you that my wife Jocasta is to be tried for witchcraft? Yes, yes. Tomorrow. Ridiculous, of course. She can't boil an egg, still less make up potions and things. Ah, well. At least the trials are fairer than they used to be.'

'Oh, yeah,' said Peter, 'so how do they go about it these days?'

'Ah, well, yes. When I was a young lad, they used to duck the poor girls in the pond, and if they sank and drowned, then obviously they weren't witches, but if they floated, they were, so they were burned at the stake. A nasty experience for a girl, that must have been, particularly at this time of the year. Powerful cold and wet, that pond. And to go straight

44

from cold to intense heat can do permanent damage to the lungs.'

'And nowadays?'

'Oh, nowadays we use the humane method. We burn them, and if their hearts burn, they are not witches, and if their hearts don't burn, they are. It's far more logical. Neater.'

'Oh, quite so,' I said, incredulous. 'Sounds as though you're gonna have a long day tomorrow, Mr Carter. You'd better go to bed.'

'But I am in bed!' Jacob Carter grinned. 'And this is a splendid dream. Nonetheless,' he yawned, 'I do feel a little tired. Perhaps I will go upstairs in my dream and see what happens. Good night, gentlemen, and thank ye very much.'

Humming happily, he pottered upstairs. We piled more wood on the fire, kicked off our shoes and sprawled wearily on chairs or on the rug.

The soft light, the moth's wing flicker of the flames and the gentle whistle of the wind outside soon silenced us. Sleep came quickly. I dreamed that I lived in a place called New York in the twentieth century.

Crazy.

Chapter Eight

I was cold again when I awoke. Egon was shaking my shoulder. His vapourized breath bounced back at him off my cheek. 'Come on,' he whispered, 'let's get goin' before our host wakes up.'

I blinked at the brightness of the light. It was a minute or two before I realized what had caused it. It had snowed in the night. I got up and stretched, then strolled over to the window whilst Egon awoke the others. I peered out.

The houses were plump with snow. The cart-ruts had vanished, though already there were deep foot-prints in the middle of the street. The sun was not quite up. It too was doing the yawning and stretching and brushing its teeth routine. There were pale layers of pink and turquoise at the horizon.

'We'd better take our uniforms and equipment down to the cellar,' Peter whispered.

'How we gonna bust ghosts without the ghostbust-ing weapons?' I demanded.

'We'll come and pick 'em up later,' he said, 'but first we've got to find the damned ghosts. That means talking to people, and if we go out there with our proton-packs, they'll be dipping us in barbecue sauce before we even open our mouths.'

We scattered our equipment around the cellar and hid it as best we could beneath the dusty bolts of fabric which we found down there. Egon kept one PKE meter which he wrapped in black cloth and carried under one arm.

We brushed down our clothes, adjusted our hats and stepped out into the snowy street.

The sun had got out of the bath now and was well-scrubbed and shiny and singing, *Oh, What a Beautiful Morning*. A cart creaked by, laden with wood.

The driver hailed us with 'Good morrow, masters,' to which Egon, who was really getting into the rôle, replied, 'God be with thee, brother.'

Opposite the tavern, a milkmaid was whistling the latest hit tune. We smiled at her and wished her 'Good morrow'. She stopped whistling and scurried quickly away.

The church stood at the top of the street. It was white and red and spick and span and the only stone building in Salem apart from the jailhouse.

'Better take a look in here,' Peter pushed open the gate in the white picket fence. 'Sounds like there might be some ghouls lurking hereabouts.'

We strolled through the sparkling graveyard and into the church. It was light and airy. The walls were white. The wooden vaulted ceiling was high. Not at all the sort of place where the layman would expect to find ghosts. We knew better.

Peter, Ray and I stood in the aisle and tried to look like we thought appreciative and respectful seventeenth-century tourists might look. Egon strolled casually around the walls with the PKE meter.

'High,' he reported on his return. 'No question. There are spooks here. I'll just try the tower.'

We nodded and admired the scenery a bit more. 'A fine example of a late baroque, er, door,' Peter pointed.

Ray nodded. 'And look at the, um, post Gothic renaissance thingamajig.'

'One of the finest I've ever seen,' I agreed. 'It reminds one of the Cathedral of Saint Barnabas in Addis Ababa, does it not?'

'Just what I was about to say . . .'

'Good morrow, brethren!' a big voice boomed from the far end of the church. We swung round. A tall man with a high brow, a hairline at low tide and a fair beard emerged from the door behind the altar. A silver cross gleamed on his chest. He leaned forward and bobbed from the waist as he walked down the altar-steps towards us. He rubbed his hands slowly together as though washing.

I knew his type at first sight. In the twentieth century, he would wear a college scarf and carry ballpoint pens in his top pocket and badges on his lapel. He would probably like electronic music and go potholing at weekends.

I glanced nervously over my shoulder. We needed Egon, fast.

'Er, God be with you, brother,' Ray held out his hand. The bearded man shook it keenly and with feeling.

'Yeah. Right. God be with you, brother,' said Peter. He got the same treatment.

Then it was my turn. His hand was soft and warm

and talcum dry. Its touch made my teeth ache. I wiped my hand on my breeches.

'Guess you're Pastor Kraft,' Ray said bravely.

'Thou speakest strangely,' the man's pale eyebrows curled in a suspicious frown. 'But indeed I am he. How knowest thou my name?'

'Doesn't everyone know the name of Pastor Kraft of Salem?' Ray grinned. We smiled and nodded as if to say, 'We speak of nothing else at home.'

It was the right response. Kraft smiled modestly and looked down at his hateful, rubbing hands. 'It is true,' he boomed, 'that the good Lord has seen fit to grant me some portion of worldly fame for my preaching and for my constant and unremitting battle against the Prince of Darkness and his minions.'

'Yeah, we wanted a word with you about that,' Peter sneered.

'Yes,' I broke in, 'we wished to congratulate thee on, er, thy excellent labours.' It helps, living with Egon.

'We did?' Peter frowned.

'We did,' I reminded him.

'I am touched, brethren,' Kraft bobbed up and down, 'though aware that it is not I who merit your felicitations but He by whose grace I am given the power to stamp out evil and evildoers, to crush them, burn them, *annihilate* them. Morning, noon and night, we must never sleep, our swords must never be sheathed, we must be eternally vigilant. Even within these hallowed walls, the dark one may

49

lurk of unseen! We must hunt it out and Kill, Kill, Kill!'

The shrieked words rang out in the vaults of the church. We looked at one another, slightly embarrassed.

'Quite so,' said Ray.

'Absolutely right,' I agreed.

'Fine Christian sentiments,' Peter nodded.

Egon emerged, breathless and dusty, from the tower. 'Well met, Pastor Kraft,' he panted. 'Thou hast a fine and stately church.' He thrust out his hand.

I closed my eyes very tight and prayed. I prayed that when I opened them again I would find myself anywhere but here in this fine and stately church. For Egon, his right hand fully occupied with holding the covered PKE meter, had offered his left – probably in itself a secret sign of witchcraft or some such. But worse, far worse than that, something decidedly un-seventeenth century glittered on his wrist.

It had started life as an ordinary wrist watch, but Egon, of course, had not been content with that. It could now tell you the time and date at any given longtitude and latitude. It contained a mini-database with information about ghosts, an alarm which could be set years in advance to tell Egon to increase the ecto-preservative gases in the containment unit, water his fungus or fetch his socks from the laundry, and countless other mysterious and totally useless functions. It was a good watch, a clever watch, the object of admiration and envy amongst his friends.

50

Here, however, it was about as suitable as a whoopee cushion at a funeral.

Peter had seen it too, I knew, because he started talking very loud and very fast about nothing, which probably made matters worse, for he seemed to be totally incapable of remembering to say 'thee' and 'thou' and 'brother' and all the other things which seemed to come so naturally to Egon.

When I opened my eyes, Kraft was still holding Egon's hand and looking straight into his eyes. I might have been imagining things, but I thought I saw an extra little glitter in the preacher's eyes, a small grim smile pulling at the corners of his mouth. 'Verily, I am honoured,' he was gushing, 'that voyagers should come hither to witness the work of the Lord's humble servant and thine here in Salem. Thou hast seen the church tower, I surmise?'

'Yea, pastor.' Egon looked down. His eyes snapped open. He snatched back his hand. His voice was a little higher as he went on. 'My curiosity was aroused for I have heard tell that it was there that the first manifestations of diabolism and sorcery occurred.'

''Tis true,' Kraft nodded keenly. 'In the midst of the holy service, harsh voices were heard to shout vile profanities. I myself was bodily knocked to the ground by an invisible hand, and night after night the bells sounded, though none was there to pull the ropes. Only sorcery could work such gross sacrilege in the house of the Lord.'

'Thinks thee not,' said Peter ungrammatically, but

doing his best, 'I mean, don't thee think that it could have been spoo – I mean, ghosts, or phantoms?'

Kraft eyed Peter as though measuring him up for the griddle. Red spots sprouted in his cheeks. His right fist clenched. 'Such talk is superstitious twaddle,' he barked sharply. 'There are no ghosts!'

'Oh, yeah?' Peter replied, 'and what about the holy variety?'

Kraft's face was becoming decidedly ugly. His knuckles looked like pawns in an ivory chess set. I stepped in. 'Yes, well, we'd love a debate about religion, but I'm afraid we just haven't got time. Got to be going, I'm afraid. Fascinating talking to you – thee, I mean – about your witches. You just keep sockin' it to 'em, vicar. Be seeing thee.'

The others mumbled farewells and turned to leave, but Kraft's voice, now deep and low, throbbed in the tiles of the floor. 'Nay,' he said softly. 'You are strangers and have come from afar. I'll not let it be said that Salem did not offer what poor hospitality it possesses, nor that the humble Pastor of Salem allowed fellow students of the occult to depart without learning something of the evildoing in this poor town. Come. You will accompany me to the tavern and there meet the Witchhunters, brave servants of the Lord and merciless purgers of all wrongdoing.'

'No, actually,' Peter smiled, 'we'd rather not, thanks.'

'But I insist, brethren.' One hand fell on my right shoulder, another on Peter's left. 'I insist.'

'Yeah,' said Peter, 'I rather thought thee might.'

Chapter Nine

The tavern was already seething when we arrived. We shouldered our way in through crowds of black-clad people. Chickens clucked and squawked at our feet. There was no bar, so we were spared the embarrassment of ordering drinks. I wouldn't have put it past Peter to have asked for a Coke.

Kraft ushered us to a large table. There were a few old people already sitting there, but Kraft merely doffed his hat at them and smiled rather nastily and expressed the wish that the Lord might smile on them and they got up quickly and joined the throng standing at the centre of the room.

There wasn't much choice in the way of drinks. You could have ale, cider, mulled wine, porter – whatever that was – or 'lamb's wool'. Kraft seemed to think that 'lamb's wool' was the suitable thing, so we all nodded and said yes, we loved a good pint of lamb's wool. We never touched anything else. Just the thing of a morning. If it wasn't for lamb's wool, where would we all be, we'd like to know.

Lamb's wool in fact turned out to be a gas. It consisted of hot spiced and sweetened beer with roast apples and bits of toast floating about in it. I'm not a beer drinker myself, but the scent of the apples and the cinnamon made it drinkable and the heat was welcome. After a while, I began to think that

Kraft had not seen Egon's watch. He merely wanted to introduce us to his pals. Alcohol dulls the brain.

The in-subject of conversation was witches. Everyone seemed to have been the last person to have talked to Jocasta, Molly or Tabitha before they were arrested, although most people claimed that they 'had always known there was something funny about her'. The tavern, apparently, was also to serve as the courtroom for the women's trial this afternoon.

Already, in the corner, a big beach-ball of a man was taking bets on the result of the trial. You could get 5,000–1 against a not guilty verdict, and 100–1 on, that the girls would be found guilty and burned. The interesting betting, however, was about whether or not they really would prove to have been witches. Public money seemed to think Molly to have the most flame resistant internal organs, then Jocasta, then Tabitha.

I was surprised to see gambling in so puritan a town. I said as much to Kraft. 'Where we come from,' I lied, 'it is regarded as sinful.'

'Indeed, it is, brother,' Kraft intoned, 'indeed it is. But all funds raised here go to the Pastor's Welfare Fund and thus, of course, to the service of the Most High. And anyhow, it is not, in the strictest sense, gambling.'

'Why not?'

'Because there is no element of chance,' he said, as though surprised that I should ask such a question. 'The evidence against these women is quite clear.'

'What evidence is that?' asked Ray.

A sudden hush fell on the room. The people

54

standing by the door drew back. Feet crunched outside. 'That,' Kraft said gleefully, 'thou shalt hear from men more qualified than I to tell you.' He stood.

The door swung open. Four men in black stepped in. Cloaks of snowflakes swirled about their shoulders. Their boots clattered on the flagstone floor. The door swung back with a bang.

'These,' breathed Kraft, 'are the Witchhunters.'

The four men plucked at the fingers of their gloves and scanned the room. 'Good morrow, brethren,' their leader bowed. The crowd said rhubarb. 'Ah, Pastor Kraft,' he removed his hat and the four men strode over to our table. 'Greetings to you.'

'May the Lord attend thy every enterprise, Master Vansittart,' Kraft gestured. 'Wouldst sit with us?'

The four men sat on the bench on the opposite side of the table. We were introduced as 'visiting scholars who have expressed an interest in recent events in Salem'. One by one, we exchanged names. More lambswool was brought. Vansittart seemed to study us very closely. We fidgeted nervously and tried to look elegant and relaxed in a seventeenth century sort of way.

'Have you come far?' asked Wilbur Zacharias.

'We come from New Amsterdam,' said Egon.

'Ah, yes. I have heard that there is a thriving little community there,' Ezra Springer blinked through steamed-up glasses. 'It was founded, of course, by Dutch settlers on the island known as Manhattan, an area of twenty-two square miles at the mouth of the River Hudson. It has, I believe, two churches and a population . . .'

'Ezra!' Piet grinned. 'These gentlemen know all that. Thou'rt a useful fund of knowledge, but a terrible gasbag.'

Richard Stert, the youngest member of the group, giggled.

'Our friends here,' said Kraft, 'are anxious to know more of your trade. They have even suggested,' he spoke through clenched teeth, 'that the dread apparitions and phenomena which have tormented this township might have been the work of – ghosts.'

There was a certain amount of chortling at this. 'Nay, nay,' Piet gave his slow, easy smile again. ''Tis a common enough fault to seek a supernatural explanation when in fact there is a perfectly natural one. Which, gentlemen, is more likely? That a witch uses the dark arts to conjure devils to her aid, or that the spirits of the dead roam this earth?'

'Well . . .' I started, but Ezra interrupted.

'Extensive research,' he bleated, 'has indicated that none of the supposed sightings of spectres, phantoms and ghouls are not susceptible to a perfectly rational explanation. Ghosts, I am afraid, do not exist, whereas, obviously, witches and warlocks do. We are living in an age of reason, brethren, free of foolish old superstition. Clear your minds of old wives' tales! Think modern! Think logical!'

'So how do you go about your business?' I asked, somewhat annoyed at being called 'old-fashioned' by someone living three centuries before me.

56

'We receive reports of strange happenings . . .' said Piet.

'We investigate and establish by scientific methods where the necromantic forces are coming from . . .' said Ezra.

'We interrogate a few people in that area, look for tell-tale signs . . .'

'And when we find 'em,' said Richard enthusiastically, 'we grab 'em. It's great.'

'What are the tell-tale signs, then?' asked Peter.

'Well, we cannot tell you too much, obviously, brother. But if someone has a lot of strange herbs in her store cupboard and is known to work cures in her community, for example, or if someone wanders forth at night for no apparent reason, or if milk or eggs placed in her parlour go sour – simple things like that – it offers grounds for suspicion at the very least.'

'But how do you actually prove it?'

'Oh, they usually make some silly error.' Piet sipped his ale. 'The devils which possess them are cunning but we must be more cunning still. Quite a lot of them confess, of course. I think, deep down, that they're glad to get if off their chests. Just an hour or two of the thumbscrew and they chatter away, really relieved and grateful to have the chance to talk to somebody about it all.'

'Nonsense,' said Peter.

Piet started. 'What!'

'Well, honestly. I mean, we all go out nights sometimes, and what's wrong with curing warts or colds or something with herbs? I've had eggs go off just because they were old when I bought them . . .'

'You have?' Wilbur's eyes narrowed.

'. . . and if you put the thumbscrew on me, I'd swear blind that I was the Boston Strangler if you asked me to. It doesn't seem very logical to me, brother.'

'So thou wouldst defend these sorceresses?' Wilbur growled. 'Mayhap you have good reason . . .'

'No, no,' Egon grovelled, 'he's just, er, making a debating point, aren't you, Peter? Just testing the strength of your faith and the efficiency of your methods, aren't you, Peter?'

Peter glared at Piet. Piet glared back, unmoved. Peter conceded.

'Yeah,' he said, 'I suppose so.'

There was silence around the table for a few seconds. No-one moved. Kraft chose his moment carefully. 'Mayhap, Master Spengler,' he purred to Egon, 'thou wouldst show my friends the curious bracelet that you wear about your wrist?'

Chapter Ten

I gulped. Something shivered in my stomach and creaked like Dracula's front door. I suddenly felt very cold again.

'No,' Egon smiled nervously, 'it's personal.'

'What has thou to hide from the Witchhunters?' demanded Wilbur.

'N – nothing!' Egon sang falsetto, 'nothing at all!'

'Why, then,' Kraft's voice was silky, 'thou'lt permit us to see thy bracelet. It is an adornment, and adornments are sinful, are they not, brother?'

'Yes,' Egon gabbled, 'of course. "Vanity of vanities, all is vanity." Very sinful. But – but, my mother asked me always to wear it. You wouldn't want me to disobey my mother, would you? And she said, very specially, that I wasn't to let anyone see it.'

'I saw it this morning,' Kraft grinned. You could hear his grin. It crackled like cellophane.

'Yes, but that was an accident.'

There was a bang and the table shook – Piet Vansittart's hand clamped down on Egon's wrist. 'Come, brother,' he said smoothly, 'thou'rt evasive.' He drew back Egon's black cuff.

There was a gasp around the table, then a knowing murmur. Piet crossed himself. 'Take if off,' he ordered.

Egon sorrowfully removed the watch. Piet held out a hand. Egon looked at each of us in turn, then dropped the golden circlet into the chief Witchhunter's hand.

'It is gold, yet is weighs less than gold,' Piet raised his eyebrows. 'Is that logical enough for thee, Master Venkmann? Is that not magic? It has mysterious numbers upon it, numbers which – by God!'

'What is it?' the Witchhunters cried.

'See! See! The numbers change even as I hold this devil's artifact! They change before my very eyes!'

The Witchhunters craned their necks to look closer at this miracle. All crossed themselves. I slid sideways on the bench.

'And see here!' Piet pointed, 'strange, incomprehensible words! Are these not a warlock's arcane incantation? Why else would they be inscribed here? See! S-E-I-K-O, and here! Q-U-A-R-T-Z! Do these very letters, these very words not fill your hearts and souls with dread and revulsion? Seiko quartz! The words rumble and resound from the depths of hell itself!'

A lot of things were happening as he raved. First, the crowd fell silent. They backed up until they stood four deep pressed up against the wall. They gazed towards our table in dread.

Second, the three other Witchhunters stood and now regarded us with wary outrage. Wilbur Zacharias stood over me with folded arms and glared warningly down at me. It was fairly clear that we were going nowhere. Nowhere, that is, save, perhaps, the jailhouse, or the stake.

'Egon,' I said as evenly as I could manage, 'show them what else your bracelet can do.'

Egon frowned at me, puzzled, then nodded. He reached out for the watch, but Piet closed his fist. 'No,' Egon said, 'I wasn't trying to take it. I just wanted . . . Why don't you press those buttons on the side? The numbers will change again.'

Piet eyed him suspiciously. 'Beware,' said Richard, who stood menacingly over Ray. 'It may be a ruse.'

'It may,' Piet grinned up at him, 'but did we Witchhunters e'er run from peril?' He pressed one button, started back and muttered a rapid prayer. 'We are seeing,' he announced, 'the ultimate in diabolical ingenuity. We are actually reading here direct instructions from the Evil One himself. "Feed *ranunculus viridis sempervivens*", it says – obviously some loathsome monster that he hath conjured. "Ring chemical supplier", A-ha! So he seeks to betray even the poor misguided soul who furnishes him with the materials of his potions! Who knows what dread tortures are meant by those words "to ring"?'

He stabbed another button, and this time the effect was dramatic and instantaneous.

Egon, I should explain, is a deep sleeper. He therefore decided to amplify the tune which his watch plays as an alarm signal. That tune just happens to be *The Yellow Rose of Texas*.

I, on the other hand, am a light sleeper. I shudder to think of the number of times when, after a hard day's work, I have been wrenched from a particularly enjoyable dream by the strains of *The Yellow*

Rose of Texas. The watch sounds like a grieving squaw, yet, time and again, Egon has slept on while said grieving squaw has shrilled *The Yellow Rose of Texas* only inches from his ears.

For this reason, I have come to hate *The Yellow Rose of Texas* with a very deep, sincere and passionate loathing. Just two notes of it are sufficient to send me into a murderous rage. First, I want to throttle Egon, then ritually disembowel the composer of *The Yellow Rose of Texas*, then stamp on every Rose and spit at every Texan until I feel better again.

For once, that homicidal feeling was going to come in quite useful. For, at the moment when Piet pressed that button and the accursed melody bounced out into the air, I moved.

Piet had dropped the watch in horror. The Witchhunters stared at it, transfixed. The onlookers whimpered and prayed. I bent down, picked up the heavy oak table and, with a grunt, flung it over.

Richard was taken totally by surprise. The leading edge of the table caught him hard on the knee and its weight threw him over backwards. Ezra had seen it coming and threw himself back. He would not be long recovering. Peter took the opportunity to turn round and punch Kraft on the pious point of his heavy jaw.

That left Piet, who had sprung from his chair with astonishing speed, and Wilbur, who had seen my initial downward movement and so had had time to get out of the way. Wilbur crouched, ready to fight.

I leaped over the table, spun him round and pushed downward with two fingers at the carotid pressure point. He sagged and rattled to the floor like a stringless puppet. To my left, Peter and Egon were fighting a losing battle against Piet and Ezra. For a second, I considered going to their aid, but Kraft was rising to his feet and a few braver members of the crowd had already armed themselves with bottles. It was time to go.

'Come on!' I yelled to Ray, 'let's get out of here!'

Ray was at my left shoulder as I charged out into the snowy street, slithering and kicking up clods of earth. We ran back towards Jacob Carter's joint. I heard yells and footsteps behind us, then the shots.

Somehow I had not expected shots. I mean, I suppose I knew that muskets existed, but I did not associate them with the calm, olde worlde charm of Salem, a charm which was frankly beginning to wear thin.

I crouched and weaved. One bullet thudded into the wooden wall of a house before me. Another kicked up a spray of snow about six inches ahead of my feet.

'Where are we going?' Ray yelled at me as the echoes died.

'I dunno. Keep running!'

We swung round a corner into a side street. The shouts of the crowd were a long way behind us now, but they would not, I knew, stop looking for us. They would search slowly and methodically, knowing that, in this weather at least, there was nowhere for us to go.

The old nag which we had seen first thing that morning still stood hitched to his cartful of wood at the end of the alleyway. He looked very shaggy and very tired. His head hung low. He chomped very slowly on something in his nosebag. I gestured to Ray. We ran over. I untethered the horse and nodded to Ray. 'You know how to drive one of these things?' I panted.

'Nope.'

'Me neither. Should be fun finding out. Hop on, and pretend to be a log.'

Ray clambered aboard the cart. I followed. There was another shout from behind us. I glanced over my shoulder. The first of our pursuers had emerged at the entrance to the alleyway. Others rapidly joined him. One of them, I noticed, carried a pitchfork.

I cursed, picked up the tether and lashed at the horse's rump. He did not seem to notice. He just kept munching.

'Garn!' I yelled. The nag turned and looked at me with an expression of sorrow mingled with disdain. A stone whistled past my right ear.

'Here!' rapped Ray behind me. He tugged a long whippy hazel branch from the pile of wood in the cart.

'Thanks,' I grinned nervously. I raised the stick and brought it down hard.

The horse stiffened in surprise, took one quick, astonished glance at me, and bolted. I fell backward and cracked my skull against the boards of the cart. My brains rattled about a bit, and by the time that I could sit up and pay attention, we were careering around another corner, tilted at an angle of forty degrees.

Ray was rolling around with the movements of the cart. He looked uncomfortable. 'Can't you steer this thing?' he screamed.

I looked around for the reins, which I had somehow neglected to pick up before setting off. I dived forward and grabbed them just as the horse swung round a left hand bend. Ray rolled to the other side of the cart, rapidly followed by a lot of logs. I was almost thrown out and hung over the edge, my head just a couple of feet from the ground.

The cart rocked back on to all four wheels. I scrabbled back on to the driver's seat. We were out of the town and climbing a steep hill now, and pine trees flashed by on both sides in a blur. I leaned back and pulled hard. It had little effect. The nag had decided that it was running in the Washington International and that the competition was only just behind.

This had to stop. It was good news, perhaps, that we were leaving our pursuers far behind, but it was decidedly bad news that we would have to trudge back many miles through deep snow if we were to rescue Peter, Egon and the girls before the people of Salem started lighting bonfires later this afternoon.

A moment later, the news became altogether worse. The road dipped down. Beneath us to the left the hill plunged sheer down for several hundred feet. There were rocks beneath the snow – large ones on the left which grated against the wheels and sent pink sparks flying, small ones in the middle which caused the cart to jolt and judder and my cheeks to shake until I could hardly see.

'R-R-R-Ray-ay!' I yelled. 'C-c-come -m-m-m he-he-he-here!'

Ray struggled forward. The sandpaper wind had buffed his cheeks to smooth, shiny hemispheres of crimson. His eyes were very wet. I handed him half of the reins, and together we leaned back and tugged with all our might. It did no good. We continued to hurtle down the narrow road towards a sharp right hand bend.

'There has to be a brake!' I called.

Ray looked around. Suddenly he ducked down and plunged to his right. He grasped a short plank of wood on the side of the driver's box and pulled.

In retrospect, I wish that he hadn't. We might not have got round that corner, I suppose. We might have plummeted to our certain doom, but at least we'd have plummeted smoothly and quietly, aside, perhaps, from a scream or two.

It was the screech and the crack and the groaning of splitting wood that I objected to, the shrieking of that damned nag, the sudden sense, later proved to be accurate, that I was being projected howling and flapping forward and that the rough, white-veiled hillside was rushing up towards me like a mouth opening into a scream.

I didn't like the fact that the hill hit me in several places in rapid succession, then cut me, tossed me about and bruised me in several of my more tender spots before depositing me on a large boulder ten yards from the spot at which I had landed. Even less did I like the fact that Ray, above me, flew in a perfect parabola and landed with his elbow in my stomach.

'Phew!' he said, 'good thing we had a soft landing.' I had to wait until I recovered my breath and stilled the chiming of bells inside my skull before I could express my opinion.

I then did so at some length and with feeling.

I'd rather not talk about our journey back to Salem, if you don't mind. Our horse, minus the cart (which was now kindling for someone's bonfire), had turned round and headed home. By the time that we caught sight of Salem church tower again, the nag was no doubt tucked up in a deep bed with a good book and a bran mash and some tall tales to tell to its grandchildren.

We meanwhile were bleeding, cold, tired, wet and bad-tempered. We also knew by the position of the sun that it must be at the very earliest two o'clock in the afternoon. Our friends had been standing trial for at least two hours.

Neither of us expected Piet's sort of justice to take long, and, as we crested that final hill, our eyes at once scanned the sky above the market place for dark columns of smoke. There were none, but we stopped our bickering at that moment.

For all our concern, caution was our first priority. We approached the town like snakes, flat on our stomachs, and darted through the deserted streets from dark doorway to dark doorway.

Our first destination was Jacob Carter's cellar. We needed that equipment. Fast.

Carter's door was locked, but that posed no problem for Ray. At least here for a moment we did not have to be nervous. Old Carter, after all, had thought us to be a dream, and as he had said, would mention that dream to no-one for fear of being thought a warlock himself. We could also presume, unless the nature of marriage had changed drastically over three hundred years, that he would stay at his wife's trial until the bitter end.

We had no time for warming up. We ran straight down to the cellar, threw off our black clothes and put our uniforms back on. We strapped on our proton-packs in silence. We slung the other two proton-guns over our shoulders.

'Feels good,' I said.

'Yeah. Church or courtroom first?'

'Church. Has to be. We came here to save those girls and get rid of Dr Armour's spooks, whatever the cost. If we go to the courtroom first, we'll get the guys out, but we'll have no chance of getting back to the ghosts. Ghostbusters are expendable, Ray.'

'Yeah,' his mouth narrowed in a humourless grin. He slapped my shoulder. 'OK. Let's go.'

We were Ghostbusters again.

Chapter Eleven

It was three o'clock when we left Carter's house.

The sun, as previously mentioned, had started the day full of optimism and promise. Men in the know had confidently predicted that it would have a bright, not to say brilliant future. And indeed, throughout the morning it had shone like crazy. It had been conscientious about its job. It had not skipped dark corners just because nobody would notice. Hardly anything had been left untouched by its work. Now, however, it was past its prime. So few people had ventured out to appreciate its efforts that it felt disillusioned and unloved. If it had known that it would have been like this, it would never had bothered to get up in the first place. It had a good mind to go to Australia for a well-earned rest, and serve us right.

Again we scurried up the street, our backs to walls. The tavern door was shut and the windows coated with a thick crust of frost, but we could hear the hubbub from inside. Kraft's voice rang above the rest. We'd had a hard time this afternoon, but I'd sooner have stayed on that cart for two hours of breakneck galloping than be where Peter and Egon were now.

We'll have to rely on their account of what was happening in there, so don't blame me if this part of the book lacks the wit and sparkle of the remainder. Some of us can and some of us can't, that's what I say. It's just nature, and there's no point in arguing with it.

A seventeenth century trial, it appears, was quite a party. The audience came from miles around. They drank lambswool and mulled wine. They cheered every good speech. They jeered and whistled and stamped and barracked and exchanged bad jokes. One of the things which baffled Peter and Egon was that the alleged witches joined in with good humour, even though the subject under discussion was whether or not they'd be Fryin' Tonite.

The judge was a little monkey of a man with a face like an old apple. He was irritable, prejudiced and stone deaf. Every so often, when a good point was made by one of the prosecutors, he would increase his bet on a guilty verdict. Peter did not find this encouraging.

First Piet Vansittart gave an opening address in which he outlined the evidence against the girls and the Ghostbusters. It was pretty damning. Not only was there all the convincing material about eggs and stuff, but our magical arrival, our strange dress and manner of speaking and Egon's watch and PKE meter more or less made it an open and shut case. We were supernatural. The girls had conjured us. Therefore the girls were witches. If, the argument went the other way, the girls were witches and we had been conjured by them, then we must be devils. Obvious.

The lawyer for the defence then lurched to his

feet. He was a big, burly, red faced man with spiky
black hair and a shiny, flopping lower lip. His name
was Amos Olsen. He worked, appropriately enough,
in the town's slaughterhouse. He had been
appointed to defend the accused because – well,
because why not? Someone had to do it, and everyone knew old Amos, and he could drink a yard of
ale with two full tankards balanced on his head.
Who better?

'Juzh,' he nodded to the judge, 'and jury. I'm here
to defend zhese wishes againsht the charges of
wishcraft. An' what I say ish, if zhey're not wishes,
how come zheyre shtanding zhere accused of wishcraft, hey? Coursh zhey're wishes. But what I shay
ish, why not? Got to have wishes, elsh who would
we burn at the shtake? 'f it weren't for whishes,
Shalem would have no tourisht indushtry . . .' he
trailed off, studied his notes, took a deep swig of his
mulled wine and swayed very slowly from side to
side. '*And*,' he suddenly boomed, 'it'sh not zhere
fault. 'cos zhey come from broken homesh an' never
had any prental guidansh an' all that . . .' he wiped
a maudlin tear from his eye and swayed some more.
'*And*,' he pointed grandly at the wall, 'can we afford
to washte good wood? It'sh gettin' cold. Lot of
wood, it takesh, wish-burning. I wan' you to conshi-
der zhat very, very . . .' he nodded smugly, aware
that he had made a telling point. 'That'sh all,' he
announced. He drew himself up to his full height,
swayed alarmingly and toppled backwards like a
felled tree, smashing the chair beneath him. There
was a lot of cheering and applause.

'An eloquent defence,' the judge rapped. 'I particularly want the jury to take note of the argument about the fish. Very important detail, that.'

'Excuse me,' Egon shouted. The crowd jeered and lobbed baked apples in his general direction. Egon stood his ground until the noise died down. 'Excuse me,' he said, 'but this is a travesty of justice. We have not been defended at all. We dismiss our counsel and will now conduct our own defence.'

'Whass he say?' the judge snapped.

'He wishes to conduct his own defence!' Piet yelled in the judge's ear.

'Well, he can't,' said the judge. 'I haven't got time to waste listening to a lot of arguing. I'm going out to dinner. I want to get home, have a bath and things.'

'He is allowed to, sir,' Piet assured him.

'Why?' demanded the judge.

'It is stated in the statute book of 1606, section 210, paragraph nineteen, sub-section C . . .' began Ezra.

'Yes, yes!' the judge slammed down his ear-trumpet, 'but not when the judge is going out to dinner! Surely that's obvious enough! Another day, maybe I'd consider it, but there's snow out there, in case you hadn't noticed.' He turned to Egon, 'Show a little consideration, young man,' he said. 'This sort of selfishness will not stand you in good stead when it comes to the verdict, you know. I want this whole thing over by four o'clock.'

'But you're talking about our lives!' Peter protested.

'Don't make trouble!' whispered little Tabitha.

Witnesses were called. Seth Goodbody's evidence

was precisely the same as in the account which Dr Armour had read to us less than twenty four hours before and more than three centuries later. Egon tried to cross-examine him but was shouted down by the mob.

Kraft came next. He surprised everyone by pleading for mercy for Jocasta, Molly and Tabitha. They, he said, were poor misguided women who had been corrupted by the power of Satan himself. They should just be burned at the stake.

For Peter and Egon, however, and for Ray and me when they caught us, there could be no such liberal soft-heartedness. We should be half hanged, half-burned, and half-drowned. Bits should be chopped off us and thrown into the fire before our eyes. If anyone had any other imaginative ideas as to how we should be shown the error of our ways he would be glad to hear them.

The crowd had lots of ideas. There was poison, of course (the excruciatingly agonizing variety), and then we could be torn apart by wild horses. Our fingernails and hair could be pulled out and we could be crushed with heavy stones.

You couldn't have hoped for a more enthusiastic and helpful audience.

Any semblance of justice had long since been abandoned. The crowd was chanting. Kraft was yelling 'Kill! Kill!' The judge grinned nastily and put the last of his money on a guilty verdict. Peter and Egon, now splattered with roast apples and ale, stood, now very pale, facing that most evil of all things on earth, a mob with just one thought. They knew that death could only now be minutes away.

73

Chapter Twelve

There were no candles in the church. The morning's brightness was now greyish and lustreless. The echoes of our voices flapped like big birds in the ceiling.

We dropped back immediately into the practised and polished routine. Ray put on his spectro-visor. I did not, so that my eyesight would be unimpaired in case anyone should creep up on us. He took the 'sniffer', I the PKE meter. We scanned the nave of the church like spaniels in search of a scent, quartering the ground, ensuring that we covered every square inch.

The results were astonishing.

Nothing.

Oh, sure, there was residual PKE of a highish level, but nothing like that which Egon had reported only hours before, and as for the ghost-detector – well, there just weren't any ghosts there.

'This is weird,' Ray straightened from beneath a pew. 'PKE can't have dropped that far.'

'Unless we've got a ghost on the loose in the streets.'

'Don't, Winston. Don't even think about it.'

'Let's try the tower.'

We clambered up a narrow wooden staircase to the belfry. It was very dark and dusty up there, and I confess that, when something soft brushed lightly against my face, I leaped back, proton-gun at the ready.

My heartbeats came slowly back to normal. Bell ropes.

'Nothing for you?' I asked softly.

'Nothing.' I shook my head, dismayed. 'You know what this means?' Ray shivered. 'What it may mean, at least?'

'Tell me.'

'That we've been wrong all along. That these guys knew a thing or two. Maybe there are witches and warlocks here. Maybe it's not as simple as ghosts. Maybe what we call ghosts in our time were once devils conjured by humans in past times. Maybe . . .'

'Maybe the sky is green and God didn't make the little green apples,' I said sharply. 'Forget it, Ray. We've met those girls and we know about ghosts. Don't talk rubbish. OK, so maybe someone has been stupid enough to dabble in the occult. We've seen it in our time. But there was a high PKE reading this morning and there isn't one now. Our spook has flown.'

'Yes.' Ray bit his lip. The high colour in his cheeks receded. 'Yes, OK. You're right.'

'Only problem is, where do we go from here?'

'Dunno,' Ray shrugged. 'We've got so little time . . .'

'We can't search each house in Salem. The guys'll be in an ashtray by then. So we have to give up on the girls, perhaps try again once we've got Peter and Egon out.'

'I don't see any other choice,' Ray said dully. 'I mean, we can probably get the girls *out* . . .'

'Yeah, but what good does that do 'em? Soon as we return to the good old twentieth century, they'll be kebabbed again.'

'Unless . . .' Ray gulped.

'Yeah?'

'Unless . . . one of us stays here.'

The import of his words sunk in. I wished it hadn't. Maybe that was what Dr Armour's history books did not record. That some weird guy who spoke funny and carried a proton-gun appeared from nowhere in Salem and imposed sanity and law by the force of the gun. That he lived here.

And died here.

The Ghostbusters had never backed off before. Never failed to finish a job once we'd started it. I'd said it to Ray only minutes ago. *'Ghostbusters are expendable.'* If we had a choice between losing one of the team or failing to bust a ghost, our duty was clear.

We were Ghostbusters, first and always.

The spring had gone out of our step as we emerged in the icy air again. Snow was falling. Flakes pattered and scattered like seeds across the ice, making us look over our shoulders again and again to see who was following us.

'Keep the "sniffer" on,' I told Ray, 'just in case it gets whiff of our missing spook.'

He nodded. We had given up hiding now. There was no point. We were headed for a showdown. We strode down the middle of the street, weapons at the ready.

The hubbub in the tavern had grown. The wooden walls seemed to shake to the growling and roaring of the crowd, the strident, ringing tones of the prosecutors. Ray and I stood on either side of the door, our backs to the clapboards. I nodded once. He gave me a weak smile.

'OK?' I whispered.

'OK. And . . . go!'

I unlatched the door and barged it open in one smooth movement. Ray tumbled through and landed neatly on his feet. I slid through behind him and covered the room as he stepped forward.

'OK!' he cried. 'One move and you're zapped, and I mean zapped good!'

The people backed away to the sides of the room with a whole zooful of sounds. There were the squeaks and whimpers of the smaller hairy mammals, barks of alarm and, more worryingly, deep, big cat growls which made the floor fizz.

Peter and Egon stood behind a small table in the far corner. They had lost their hats, and their black suits wore a glossy coating of green. They looked cold and dispirited. A burly gaoler stood on either side of them. In the opposite corner stood the three girls in their ragged clothes, the defiant glare of cornered animals in their eyes.

The judge and Pastor Kraft sat at the same long table at which we had sat this morning. The Witchhunters, who had been sitting against the right hand wall, were already on their feet. They looked ready for action.

'Peter!' called Ray. He threw the spare proton-gun. Peter caught it and backed out from behind the table, keeping the gun towards the Witchhunters, his back to the wall. Egon followed. They joined us at the centre of the room. I handed Egon his gun and we lined up, our guns covering the whole room.

The Witchhunters lined up opposite us and walked slowly towards us, their black gloved fingers flexing.

'Back off!' I commanded.

They paid no attention. Piet's lips curled in an ironic smile. Ezra glared fixedly through his glittering glasses. Wilbur – who looked the stupidest of the lot as far as I was concerned – walked almost sinuously, his hips thrust forward. A broad, innocent, open grin grew on Richard's chubby face.

'Better show 'em we're not joking!' Ray called. 'The table?' he asked.

'The table,' we nodded.

We turned towards the judge and the preacher. We fired. It took about half a second for the ions to slice through the table legs. The heavy tabletop fell to the floor with an almighty crash. The judge, leaped to his feet gibbering. 'Outrageous! This is outrageous!' Kraft stood flattened against the wall. He sneered, but his pale skin was paler and something pulsed at the side of that high brow.

'Devil's work!' he roared, 'instruments of the evil one. Do not fear them! Kill! Kill! Kill!'

The crowd growled as if to express their agreement, but did not seem too keen to do anything about it just yet. In fact, a few of them seemed to

78

have developed headaches and thought they had better go home and lie down.

The Witchhunters glanced at one another, uncertain. 'This may take longer than we thought,' said Piet.

'Too right, son,' drawled Peter, 'because if you take one more move, we'll saw you in half just like those table legs. You dig?'

They seemed to understand. They nodded slowly.

'OK, back up against the wall. Girls, come over here!'

The girls looked as frightened of us as anyone else, but they had little choice. They clung to one another behind our backs, probably thinking that burning wasn't so bad really.

'Now listen, and listen good,' said Peter. 'We ain't witches or warlocks or anything like that, and nor are these good ladies. What you've got in this town is a few straightforward ghosts, and my friends here have zapped them, haven't you, guys?'

'Uh-uh,' I whispered in Peter's ear.

'Oh, God,' he murmured. He took a deep breath. 'What we're facing here is stupidity and ignorance and superstition and evil – yes, there is evil here, but the evil is in *you*, not in the people that you accuse. It is the evil of fear, which makes people so anxious to avoid blame that they have to put it on someone else. You know that these women aren't witches. You know that you have made infusion of herbs yourselves, had addled eggs in your kitchens, had dogs and cats run away from you, performed strange, superstitious rituals for good luck or to see who you're going to marry or to make sure you get a good crop this year. Of course you have! We all have! But when something goes wrong, you instantly pretend that you haven't and that it's this or that evil person to blame. It's easier that way, isn't it? Easier than accepting that there is good and evil in all of us and that bad things can and will and *should* happen by the law of nature. Oh, yeah, sure. It's easier to burn someone, then you can relax and say, "Right, we've dealt with that". Don't you see what you're doing? You're using these women as lucky charms! You're more witches and warlocks than they are! You burn them, as though by doing so you can stop earthquakes and storms and snakebites and bad harvests! And you're encouraged to do so by evil, mischievous, bloodthirsty, power-crazed men like this man,' he pointed dramatically, 'this so-called man of God who does murderous mischief in your community and so serves Satan and not God! He is the imp in your midst! Pastor Kraft!'

Peter's shoulders slumped. He looked around as though expecting applause. He probably even had an encore ready, but unfortunately, the audience did not seem to like his act. They just growled a little bit more.

Kraft strolled casually into the middle of the room. 'Typical,' he sighed. 'Typical of the glib arguments of the devil's servants. Have ye not noticed that witches always sound logical and persuasive, while the true servant of the Lord is a simple man who speaks simply and from the heart, not the head? This man and his fellows have shown you dreadful

80

magic, have a thousand times demonstrated that they possess unearthly and unnatural powers, and now they plead for these handmaidens of Beelzebub, saying there are no witches! Ha! Are ye angels, then?' he scoffed. 'Is this the sort of company that we can expect to keep when we move on to our heavenly reward? Where are their wings? Where their sweet voices? And if they are not angels, and have shown that they are not mere mortals, what else can they be but devils incarnate? Heed them not, my brethren, but Kill! In the name of the good Lord and of all that is holy, Kill, Kill, Kill!'

Chapter Thirteen

This proved a more popular act than Peter's. The crowd moved in. A bottle narrowly missed my head. The catchphrase, 'Kill, Kill, Kill!' spread rapidly through the crowd. We fired a couple of rounds at their feet and they drew back, but it could only be temporary. Sometime soon they would muster their courage and charge. And we, of course, would not be able to resist. Ghostbusters do not kill the innocent or the ignorant.

'Friend Peter,' Piet stepped forward, his hand upraised. 'Thou sayst much which is true. Thou touchest upon many concerns which have sore worried us in our quests for witches. Pray tell me, then, in answer to our Pastor, if thou'rt neither angel nor devil, what art thou?'

'We are men from another age.' Peter glanced nervously from side to side. 'We have come from the future to bring justice to this town. These "instruments of the devil" as you call them, are just the weapons and tools of our age. If you took your muskets back to the thirteenth century, they'd call you warlocks, wouldn't they?' Ray tapped my arm. I turned irritably and said 'Sh!'

'That "bracelet" you confiscated this afternoon was just a watch. It tells the time and the date . . .'

Ray tapped my arm again. I frowned. 'What is it?'

He jumped eagerly up and down and pointed at the 'sniffer'. I glanced down at the dial. The reading was 192 mcp and way into the red zone.

I looked quizzically at Ray. He shrugged and indicated the direction in which the nozzle pointed. My eyes followed the line.

The machine pointed directly at Pastor Kraft.

I grinned very broadly and nudged Egon. He looked, then struck his forehead with the heel of his hand as though cursing himself for his stupidity. Very, very slowly, he freed the ghost-trap from my shoulders. He nodded.

'Ladies and Gentlemen!' I shouted. Peter looked around, angry at the interruption. 'We have discovered your ghost!'

'Do not heed them longer!' Kraft roared. 'These devils can talk forever. They can persuade you of any . . .'

He shut up then, because I swivelled my proton gun and gave him a blast square in the chest. He was flung backward against the wall, his face twisted with pain and fury.

'You saw what this gun could do to solid oak,' Egon cried above the screaming of the crowd, 'so how come it does no harm to your precious pastor?'

'It is a trick!' Kraft shrieked like rusty metal. 'A trick! Destroy them *now*!'

Peter swung round to protect our backs, and all three of us turned on Kraft and let him have it. He writhed and jerked, bared his teeth and foamed at the mouth. The crowd was bellowing in fury and terror now.

We kept firing. Kraft crouched by the wall, covering his head and backing away from us. We moved round, manoeuvring him away from the wall and towards the ghost-trap.

Suddenly he stood upright, snarled and let out a roar that silenced the crowd. He tottered towards us, his body jerking as the ions hit him. His beard sprouted like liquid from a colander. His flesh turned an eery, irridescent pink. His body swelled like a balloon, ripping the black garments which had enclosed him. His mouth opened wide to reveal teeth like golf tees. Grotesque warts appeared all over his skin. He was at least four times bigger now than he had been as Kraft. We knew him now. We fired at him with glee.

The great Pastor Kraft was nothing but a common-or-garden troll.

There was pandemonium all around us. The door had been flung open and the crowd had poured screaming out into the snow. Peter was freed to add his firepower to ours. That was the decisive factor. The troll's whole huge bloated form twisted, his claws scratching vainly at the air, his throat open in a gargling roar of anger. He remained poised above the ghost-trap for a second, then his revolting form faded in blotches like an ancient photograph and was sucked into the trap.

There was silence.

'Excuse me,' Peter gulped. 'I've got to find a toilet.'

Trolls always have that effect on Peter.

Only now did I notice that the Witchhunters were still leaning casually against the wall.

'That,' I panted, 'is the end of your troubles.'

'What exactly was that creature?' asked Ezra.

'A troll,' Egon sighed and packed up the ghost-trap. 'They are probably the most mischievous of all spectral manifestations and are capable of metamorphosis.' ·

'That's shape-changing to you and me,' I told Wilbur.

'They delight in causing humans to harm one another,' Egon sighed, 'as you have seen.'

'So those women . . .?' Piet moaned.

'Were not witches. No.'

'Oh, God,' Richard clutched his brow. 'We have done evil.'

'No, no. Evil has been done to you. You were deceived. You were just the troll's instruments. Given the limits of your knowledge, you did your duty bravely. We'd have done the same.'

Peter returned from a back room, still looking faintly bilious. He and Egon returned to the Carters' house to change their clothes and pick up their proton-packs.

Ray and I sat down for a tankard of lambswool and a chat with the Witchhunters. They were quite decent guys, really, though I never could quite bring myself to like Wilbur. Ray, funnily enough, said the same about Richard. I thought he was quite cute. Egon said afterwards that he found Ezra 'excessively loquacious and grandiloquent' . . . which means that he talked too much.

Peter liked Piet best.

Egon and Peter returned with the girls. Jocasta shook our hands. Molly embraced us warmly. Tabitha giggled and hid behind the door.

'Come on, guys,' Egon tightened his proton-pack harness. 'We've got to get back to the jailhouse, and fast.'

'How do ye return to your time?' Piet asked.

'Oh, that's easy,' I grinned. I held open the tavern door to allow the girls to pass through. I caught sight of the expression on Egon's face. I gulped. 'Isn't it?'

'I don't know,' Egon frowned. 'Now that the girls are no longer distressed, the door in the continumm which they opened may close. It may already be closed. I just don't know. I have no experience of this sort of thing.'

Our pace increased quite noticeably as we strode back towards the little stone jailhouse.

The seventeenth century was all very well in its way, but there was a shortage of life's little essentials: hot and cold running water, for example, and central heating, and pizzas and the Rams and the Dodgers and Stevie Wonder and wall-to-wall carpeting and late night movies starring Debbie Reynolds. And then there was Janine, and even, I had to admit, Slimer. It seems ridiculous to think that you could miss a pistachio-coloured spook, but I think that I would have hugged him if he had turned up in Salem at that moment. Or bought him a burger at any rate.

Various heads appeared at various windows and vanished as soon as we turned to look at them. We strode swiftly into the jailhouse, ignoring Seth Goodbody's resentful objections.

Chapter Fourteen

Once more we were in that damp and mouldy tunnel. Peter tried the door of the cell. It was locked.

'Goodbody!' Piet bellowed. 'Come hither and be quick about it!'

Seth arrived, his black beard working furiously this way and that like a porcupine trying to wriggle out of a paper bag. He was plainly one of the Salemites who had been looking forward to a display of human Roman Candles. He unlocked the door and stood back to allow us in.

The Ghostbusters' flashlights came on almost simultaneously. The walls glistened like one huge slugs' trail. The girls, naturally enough, chose to stay outside in the corridor, but the Witchhunters joined us in the tiny cold room.

The beam of Peter's flashlight swung upward. We all sighed. What had seemed a staircase when we arrived proved on inspection to be some sort of buttress or ancient chimney breast. The steps led up to nothingness.

I have never been so happy to see nothing in my life.

'Quick.' Egon said softly. He swung round and shook hands with each of the Witchhunters in turn. 'Be careful,' he said, 'and take care of these people. When in doubt, assume that ignorance is your enemy.'

'Yea,' Piet nodded slowly. 'We have learned much of ye, brethren. God speed.'

'God speed,' said Peter solemnly and, with a wave at the girls, turned to follow Egon.

'Yeah, nice meeting you,' Ray slapped Ezra's shoulder. 'I'd leave you this flashlight only you can't get batteries and you'll be accused of being a warlock. Sorry. Tell you what – when you hop the perch, whyn't you haunt us? It'd be fun to fight with you guys again.'

'We'll do our best,' Piet's deep voice throbbed. 'Good bye, young'un.'

Ray too waved to the girls and blew Tabitha a kiss. He too stomped wearily up the stairs. First his head disappeared, then his shoulders, then his torso, then his legs. Each in turn dissolved and became darkness.

I was left alone in the past.

'Right,' I said slightly nervously. 'I must be goin' too. Thanks for everything, guys. Glad we're not gonna have any more witches brewed up.'

Suddenly Piet grasped my arm and held me tight. 'I would go with you, friend,' he said.

'And I,' said Ezra.

'And I,' Wilbur nodded. 'For when did we Witchhunters spurn an adventure when once it was offered? And is this not the greatest adventure that yet we have encountered?'

'Ay,' said Richard. 'To live in the future, where all men, even unto the humblest, have power such as thine . . .'

I tried to picture the four Witchhunters in New

York. I found it difficult. Of one thing I was certain. They would not like New York and New York would not exactly take to them.

'No,' I said. I pulled free of Piet's grasp and walked to the foot of the steps. 'I'm sorry, but it's impossible.'

'How so?' Wilbur demanded. 'Hast thou not travelled to our time? Why then should we not do likewise?'

'Look, I've got to go,' I said. I started to climb. 'I'm sorry, but I've got no time to argue . . .'

I stopped because Piet was already on the bottom step and the other witch-hunters were lined up to follow him. 'Listen,' I pleaded, 'You can't come! First, you haven't got social security numbers, and second . . .' I spoke faster as the truth became clear, '. . . second, you can't come because you'd be ghosts! Don't you see? Somewhere in the twentieth century your bodies lie dead and buried and rotten. You can't have two bodies, can you? So as you pass through this door, your bodies will become three hundred and fifty years old and fall to pieces and your spirits will pass through, and then you'll just be spooks and we'll have to bust you! If you follow me any further, you will die! Don't you understand?'

Piet stopped. He frowned. He turned and looked querying at Ezra. Ezra considered, then nodded, resigned.

'OK?' I urged. 'You won't follow me?'

'Nay, friend,' Piet smiled, 'be on thy way and fare thee well.'

I grinned quickly back and turned with relief to

take the last two visible steps. 'Farewell!' I called dramatically.

Then I said 'Ow.'

I had hit my head on solid stone.

I felt my head first, then the ceiling. My hands struck feverishly, furiously at the cold wet stone above me. A sort of whimper corkscrewed up from deep within me and seeped through my lips. 'No . . .?' I moaned. 'No . . .'

I was still groping and scratching and striking at the ceiling long after I knew the truth. The door had closed.

I rested my forehead on the damp wall then and, I confess, tears burned my eyes, burst and trickled down my cheeks. A huge sob shook my shoulders. I clenched my fist and pummelled at the wall.

This was not, perhaps, exactly heroic behaviour. I apologize, but be honest, can anyone out there put his hand on his heart and say that he has been stuck alone in another century and that he shed not a single tear? Did you too not think of your friends and of Debbie Reynolds and of hot baths and find that some few sobs bubbled up within you? Can you honestly assert that, when it happened to you, the prospect of eternal solitude in an alien world left you unmoved? Frankly, I doubt it.

At last I slumped down on the steps and turned tear-smeared, blinking eyes on the room below.

Piet gazed up at me and for a moment I thought that I saw pity in his eyes, then suddenly they hardened and became cloudy porcelain. 'Ha!' he boomed. 'At least we have one of them! They breed not good brains in the twentieth century, it seems. Fools!' he shepherded the other Witchhunters out of the cell. 'The holy fire will not be denied. Tomorrow morning thoult burn on earth. Tomorrow night thoult burn in hell!' He slammed the door. Before I could move, the lock had grated and clicked. His voice continued to ring in the tiny stone room. 'Didst think we were deceived by thy specious talk? How can men travel the centuries unless they be warlocks? Such power is denied mortals. Oh, aye. No doubt thou couldst open thy prison with yon devil's gun, but be mindful that twenty muskets will be directed at the door of this cell and twenty more at the door of the jailhouse. Thoult die as soon as thou stepst from thy prison. Now, think on thy sins, devilspawn, and repent, for tomorrow thoult perish as must all who serve the Evil One!'

I blinked, uncomprehending, at the little peephole in the door, and realized that, however bad living in the wrong century might have seemed, it was nothing like as bad as dying in the wrong century. For all my earlier grief and desolation, somewhere at the back of my mind I had known that I could at least live here, find friends, enjoy power. Now even that was denied me. I was to die a common criminal, unmourned and unremembered.

At first anger saved me from the depths of grief and self-pity. At least, I thought, I could take a few of the self-righteous, treacherous Witchhunters with me. Then sense crept back into my brain and took away even that consolation. Revenge would serve no purpose. It would only increase the hysterical hatred of witches and warlocks.

This was it. This was the end.

Would Dr Armour one day find a manuscript recording the mysterious warlock who had died in the flames in Salem? Would she show it to my fellow Ghostbusters so that they would know of their colleague's fate? It was unlikely. They would mourn me a little, perhaps, but would console themselves with the thought that somewhere, in a different time-zone, I was living the life of a lord. They'd pass around the coke cans and drink cheery toasts to me wherever I was and they'd gratefully switch over from Debbie Reynolds to stupid Westerns.

This last thought was altogether too much for me. I stretched out full length on the steps, turned towards the wall, covered my face and cried like a baby.

OK. OK. Not heroic. We've been through all this. I'm not proud of it, but you just try it someday and see how it feels. And when you've only got twelve hours to live and no-one that you care about is even born yet, who do you want to impress?

'Look up, Winston,' said the deep voice from the door. I ignored it and told it to go away.

'Look up, friend,' insisted Piet's voice. 'We have opened your door again.'

I rolled over, incredulous, suspecting a trick. At first my eyes were misted and I could see nothing above my head. I rubbed them with my sleeve and then I could see *nothing* above my head. No stone, no mould, no – nothing. Just total darkness.

'The door still had to be there,' purred Piet. 'we just had to make thy desire to pass through intense enough to open it again. Go, master Winston. Rejoin your friends.'

A last, high-pitched sob of joy forced its way from my mouth. I stumbled to my feet, laughing. 'Thanks, guys!' I called, and scrabbled up the stairs. 'Thanks to all of you, and good luck!'

Then I was once more in the cold, sawing wind and my hands touched wood. I pulled myself up. Brilliant light suddenly blinded me. I had to cover my eyes. Strong hands grasped me beneath my shoulders and pulled and I was sitting on the bare boards of that little attic room in Dr Armour's apartment block. There were no moans this time, only the rustling of the guys' clothing, the consoling murmur of their voices. The lights were back on. The spooks that we could not bust had returned to their own time and were alive and well. Their spirits had found peace.

We had returned only a few seconds after we had climbed into the oak chest. It was still night. Dr Armour still waited for us at the basement apartment of her friends the Greys. We had lived a whole extra twenty-four hours and, in my case at least, added ten years to my age, but the clock hand had not moved more than a few millimetres.

The most annoying thing about this was that the guys did not believe my story. Because everything that happened back there in Salem took no twentieth century time at all, it seemed to them that I had emerged just half a second after Ray. At last Egon admitted that 'it was just possible' that I might have been detained in Salem, but Peter still gives me funny, knowing looks whenever the subject comes up.

Epilogue

Egon left his watch in the seventeenth century, which is going to give some archaeologist a bit of a surprise one day, and which caused Egon a lot of aggravation when he tried to claim the insurance.

We told Dr Armour our story the following day. She checked out a few names in her files.

Piet Vansittart, it appears, became mayor of Salem. His wife's name was Tabitha, though her maiden name is not known. They had twelve children, and Piet took up writing plays. The plays were about ghosts and gore and were not, apparently, very good.

Ezra became a weirdo who wrote long and complicated books about time and the significance of numbers, so maybe he took Egon's watch apart, and an archaeologist isn't going to get a surprise after all.

Richard Stert took Holy Orders and became Pastor of Salem.

Wilbur did nothing important. He just vanished without trace.

The Witchhunters were history.